I0547184

Mary Ann, A Friend

Jack Darnell

Author of Finally Love

Copyright © 2014 Jack Darnell

All rights reserved.

ISBN:0981950752
ISBN-13:978-0-9819507-5-4

DEDICATION

To a Friend Jo Ann Trull

Jo Ann has been one of my strongest supporters, always encouraging and is always sure there is one more book up there, "Find it!" She says. Jo Ann brings a smile into many lives.

This is a work of fiction. Any reference to persons living or dead is coincidental, except for Mary Ann. Mary Ann is very real and a dear friend. She does live in the mountains but to my knowledge has never been kidnapped.

ACKNOWLEDGMENTS

I Want to thank the many friends on the internet who continually encourage my writing. Of course in the words of my friend, the REAL Jack Darnell who publishes under the name of H. Jack Darnell. He said to me: "I would write if no one read it."
I have the same feelings.

I especially want to thank Sherry, my lovely wife of over fifty eight years. She is always supportive and endures the late hours I spend with my other love, a book.
Thanks go to my Grand Children who flattered grandpa many times after a bed time story with the plea, "Just one more story grandpa."

Foreword

Mary Ann, a senior citizen and a widow, is enjoying life. Her world is filled with happiness because she has once again found love. That new world is shattered, turned upside down by an event she never in her life imagined could happen, she is kidnapped by a man barging into her life on the mountain at Greening Heights. It cannot be for money, hate or sex. For a while she is in the dark as to the reason for such a horrific event. Then she meets Andrew, a business man he declares. Mary Ann is reduced in his eyes to a Commodity.

CHAPTER 1

THE PHONE CALL

"What is it, sweetheart?"

Sherry stood silhouetted against the glass doors that opened to the pool, staring at the landline she held in her hand as if it were a foreign instrument. No reflex action, not indicating she heard Jerry. He asked again, "What is it, honey?" Still no reaction. Jerry crossed the room and put his arm around her shoulder. She jerked, and then smiled.

"What did you say darling?"

"I asked, 'what is it?', and you are standing here staring at the phone as if you have never seen one."

"I was talking to Mary Ann. Or I thought I was. She sounded so strange. It is probably my imagination but she sounded like she was afraid, worried, distant or something. I just can't place it, but it wasn't the normal Mary Ann."

Sherry and Jerry were in their home in Pittsburg. Their late-in-life marriage had been the best thing either had ever enjoyed. Many times they asked themselves, "Why did we have to wait until we were in our seventies to be this happy?" Both were doctors by profession. In the preceding years, they had both lived lives that started on the same paths but had diverged. Jerry had gone on to fame as the Head of Duke Medical, and never married. Sherry, on the other hand, had married a fellow student at Duke. She and her husband had been very successful in a small clinic in Huntersville. At least she had thought so, until things turned tragic.

Jerry had dropped out off the medical radar without explanation. He resigned as head of Medical at Duke and became a member of one of the CIA's Black Ops covert groups; he became famous within the ranks known as Doc. After many operations, he went through a tough time mentally and actually became a street person for a few years—the emotional strain resulting from the loss of a child during one of the Black Operations. He was never what could be termed a 'bum' because he came from a very wealthy family, and never wanted for the basics, although he lived in a sort of cave deep in the woods. Kids in town had tagged him with the name 'Rags'.

Then, one day, an accident involving a young boy had required all of Jerry's medical skills; the incident shocked him back to reality. He returned to the family business but was still not satisfied and needed more. He had always wanted to 'right the wrongs' in the world, so using his family wealth, he formed what he called the MVA—Modern Vigilante Association. The MVA did in fact work for right, but did in fact bend a few rules to bring justice to some who had used loop holes to continue a dirty business.

The situation that brought the lives of Jerry and Sherry back together, long after their earlier acquaintance at university, was a violent incident in which Jerry's team was forced to take the life of Sherry's first husband. Using the medical clinic, Sherry's husband, Dr. Brady Oxnard, had surreptitiously built a money laundering unit for a drug cartel. Sherry had felt for a long time that something was wrong, but she was so involved with her patients, it did not register.

The apparent crime was never solved but after the death, all the facts came out and Dr. Sherry was cleared of all wrong doing. But of course the practice was destroyed. Jerry had liked and admired

Sherry during their time in school and for a while even carried a crush, but his drive in medicine left no time for romance. And now, having interfered in her life, no matter how noble the cause, the situation bothered him. Finally, he asked his Corporate Attorney, Dallas, to arrange a meeting. At the meeting, and after a very painful explanation, Jerry said, "That is the whole story, Sherry. I hope you can forgive me. I guess I had better go now."

To his pleasant surprise, Sherry asked him to stay for more talk and she related her side of an unhappy marriage, one that was supposed to be the 'perfect' combination. It was far from it. From that time, Jerry made regular flights from his headquarters in Pittsburg to the small town of Mt. Bell to see and court Sherry. He finally proposed, she accepted, and they had a wonderfully different wedding, due to Jerry's crew pulling a fast one on the couple. BUT, it was a great wedding. This marriage of the old bachelor Jerry and the beautiful widow Sherry did make the storybook couple. They were so much in love that the disagreements were always worked out because of such a strong, endearing love.

Now, holding a wife just shaken by a phone conversation was a little unnerving. "Since the death of her husband, Mary Ann has bounced back.

She has been her old, fun-loving self again. A woman who has so much love to give, she exudes happiness, she always has. I have NEVER seen her down. Even when her husband knew his time was short, she never gave up that smile and positive attitude," she continued.

Jerry had met Mary Ann, the tall, slender, silver-haired lady with a perpetual smile that reflected in her eyes. Mary Ann and Sherry were childhood friends, spent time together in school and then, in church, which was a big part of their lives. Sherry had wanted a career as a nurse and Mary Ann had always wanted to be a homemaker and a mother. She was a natural in the kitchen and on the sewing machine, which at the time, in the 1950s, were traits admired and desired in a Southern lady. The desire in Mary Ann was so strong that she quit high school and married the love of her life. Soon, the children she had wanted so intensely came along. Her life was never boring or easy, but they got by. Along with being the homemaker, she took in work, sewing and laundry, to augment their income.

Her home was always decorated beautifully with the latest style and design in curtains. Her children sported clothes that matched any store bought gear. During that time, Sherry was pursuing her dream in the medical profession, the nurse idea behind her, for now she was going to be a doctor. She and Mary Ann were regulars in each other's lives. Sherry watched her friend's brood grow. Two girls and a tough guy proved enough, and Mary Ann had called a halt and suggested a vasectomy. Sherry had shortened Mary Ann's name to Ma. That is what the baby boy called her.

Over the years, Mary Ann had put aside some savings every month. Finally, the family was able to build a nice home in the mountains. In Sherry's mind, Mary Ann's house was just too far out, since Caleb's death especially, but as long as the phone worked to keep Mary Ann in touch, the solitude fit her to a 'T'. Along with her sewing she had taken up crocheting, everyone seemed to have one of Mary Ann's Afghans, at no cost.

Now, in the autumn of their lives, the girls were still very close. Mary Ann's children were grown with families of their own. She had taken care of her husband, who was a little demanding up until the last. Then, she worked her way through the loss of her husband. After that, she even acquired a suitor. The two girls joked about having a ball in their later years. Normally, after a phone call, Sherry was all smiles, sharing with Jerry the latest romantic girl talk over their favorite coffee.

"I had hoped she would move off the mountain. That is too far out for a single woman, especially at our age."

"What did she say specifically that bothers you?"

"It wasn't exactly what she said, but the tone. You know those mechanically generated voices." Jerry nodded. "It was like I was talking to a machine. I asked if anything was wrong, and she said the strangest thing. She said, 'No sweetie, I guess I am just missing Calbie. You know how sweet and understanding he always was."

"Well?"

"Honey, she never called him Calbie. I have never even heard her utter that word and he was not ALWAYS sweet and understanding."

Jerry knew Sherry was very concerned, but he was not about to fan the flames from five hundred miles away. "Well, sweetheart, maybe in tomorrow's phone call you will learn more. She could be feeling bad. Buck might not have showed up for a date and she doesn't want to talk about it right now."

"You are probably right. Of course she has the right to be down sometimes. It is just so odd."

"We can talk about this later if you want; right now, let's go to dinner. Mama has fixed my Southern favorite, chicken and dumplings. She got the recipe from a lady named Susie." Jerry always referred to his cook as Mama. Chicken and dumplings was not Sherry's favorite but she wouldn't turn it down; besides, she had to smile at the mention of her mother, Susie.

The mood was jovial at the dinner table, as always. Mama could put anyone at ease. At her job, she had entertained a prince, top politicians and paupers. After being seated, the meal was served. "I know you are not partial to the dumplings ma'am, so I fixed you some fresh salmon stew." Mama smiled as she placed the bowl in front of Sherry.

"Do you know everything, Mama?" Sherry asked, laughing.

"What that lady doesn't know, she will finagle or lie to find out," Jerry said.

"Now Mr. Jerry, you shut your mouth. I ain't never lied!"

"See, there is proof," Billie (Mama's husband) said as he walked into the table carrying a big bowl of chicken and dumplings for his dinner.

Sherry was still amazed. She had never expected to know a billionaire, much less marry one. The ultimate amazement was he preferred the staff to eat at the table with them because he looked at them as family. No one had a bigger heart than this man she had married. The warmth and family atmosphere put Mary Ann's phone call in the background.

"The dumplings are fantastic. You know Daddy always said you were a magician in the kitchen, I think I am beginning to believe it."

Mama smiled at the deserved compliment.

"You would think she was more bossy than magician, iffen you wuz married to her," Billie said in mock fear without looking up.

"Yeah, the man in you says that now, but you do remember it is your time to do the dishes," Mama said in matched mock seriousness. Then they all laughed.

After dinner, Mama served coffee and some stacked apple pie, another recipe compliments of Susie. Sherry could not get over how everyone went overboard to welcome her into the family. At times, there were lots of jokes about Jerry searching so long to find the right woman that he almost waited too late. This home in Pittsburg was the one Jerry grew up in. He also grew up with the staff, and they were all like family.

The two of them had agreed to make Mt. Bell, Sherry's hometown, their main residence. No staff, just a comfortable place to live. But usually, once a month, they flew to Pittsburg and enjoyed time there.

Jerry still kept his plane. Over the last couple of years, the pilot had changed. Elsie Mae had been Jerry's pilot for years. She was now flying for Delta airlines, 'moving the big stuff,' she said. The latest pilot was also a female and very good at the job, Stella had won out over several, and probably the final decision was made with Elsie's recommendation of Stella. They were cousins, Stella a little younger than and not quite as feisty as Elsie had been. Vickie was still the mechanic and of course, her friendship with Stella had aided in Jerry's decision to hire his new pilot.

As was their practice, Jerry and Sherry went for a walk after dinner. The estate was large enough for them to get a few miles in circling it a couple of times. It was a very pleasant evening and the phone call returned to Sherry's mind. "That talk with Mary Ann still bugs me. When we get back, I am going to call her again. I cannot get this off my mind for some reason."

"Sounds like a plan, honey. I know it would be hard to sleep if you didn't get something settled in your mind."

As the walk continued, they were caught up in their own thoughts. The walking path took them past the nice home where Mama and Billie still lived and where they had raised their family. Jerry's dad had built it at the same time the mansion for his family was built. It was always fun to see the wild life this close in to Pittsburg. At times they even saw a white tail bound off out of sight.

As they approached the house, the lights were being turned off, except for the outside, kitchen and their bedroom area. The staff was calling it a night. There would be hot chocolate and the ever present sticky buns available, if they wanted them.

They sat at the kitchen table, the one Jerry remembered fondly from his childhood. Sipping the hot chocolate, Sherry took out her cell phone and hit speed dial for Mary Ann.

After eight rings, a recording, Mary Ann's voice strained as before, "I will be out of town for a few days. Leave a message at the beep. I will return your call." Followed by a pause and a beep.

"Hello Mary Ann, this is Sherry. Please call as soon as you can. Love you, girl." After disconnecting, she again stared at the phone.

"I assume you were leaving a message, so you got no answer?"

"You assume right, and in a strained voice again she said she would be out of town for a few days and would return the call. Jerry, what could be wrong?"

"You tell me, sweetheart. You have great intuition. I have grown to trust it more and more."

"Well, something is wrong. I have no idea how serious. I hate to start a problem when there is none. I don't want to call her family this time of night, but I can call Buck just to see if maybe he and she have eloped or something," Sherry said, trying to smile and inject some humor, but she felt none. "Hey, am I brain dead? I will call her cell number."

Quickly hitting the speed dial, the phone rang and rang. She was about to give up when a hesitant voice said, "Hello, who is this?"

Startled but quickly recouping, she said, "This is Dr. Wiley, trying to reach Mrs. Mary Ann Kirkman. To whom am I speaking?"

"Hey doctor, this is Johnny Thomas. I live up near Lenoir. A while ago I was walking home from my girl's house and this pickup goes by and this phone fell out or was dropped. I just found the battery and put it back together when it started ringing and it was you."

Flipping the speaker on, she placed it on the table. "What road, Johnny?"

"Zack's Ford. Are you really a doctor and a lady, too?"

"Yes Johnny, what color was the pickup?"

"It was pretty dark, but I think it was black, but I do know it was a Hummer pickup, because that is what I want when I get my license."

"I would like to return Mary Ann's phone to her. Where can I get it, that is, where do you live?"

"We live in lot ten at the trailer park."

"Is that the trailer park just after I turn on to Zack's Ford Road?"

"Yes, ma'am."

It might be late tonight or tomorrow before someone comes to pick it up, do you think that will be okay?"

"I guess so. The furniture factory cut back and Dad is laid off. He is usually home 'cause Mama takes the car to work. 'Course I will be in school probably."

"Well, you can count on a reward for finding that phone. Thank you so very much, Johnny."

"Wow, I never got a reward before. Thanks. Good night, doctor."

"You heard. Now what do you think?"

Jerry's mind was running a mile a minute. This was a lot to digest, but something could definitely be wrong. Then, many times, things are not what they seem. "Do you know of any one Mary Ann knows with a Hummer?"

"No, her son has a pickup but it is a customized 1955 Ford and it's white. Could she be in trouble and, upon seeing this kid, dropped her phone out the window?"

"That is definitely one scenario. Another is someone may have stolen her purse and was getting rid of the phone. Some phones can be traced by GPS."

"My Lord, Jerry, if they stole her purse, where is she?"

"Don't panic yet. You were about to call Buck. Call him."

Buck was not on speed dial. She was looking in her purse for the number. Mary Ann had given it to her, but she had never called it. She had met Buck only once. Across the table, she saw Jerry take out his phone and dial. She lost her concentration when she heard Jerry say, "Sorry to bother you, Stella, but we may need to fly to Charlotte in a bit. Can you handle it?" He paused. "Yeah, I know it was a silly question. Give you a call in a few. Thanks, lady."

Sherry found the number and dialed. "Hello,

Buck here, your dime my time."

Smiling in spite of herself, Sherry said, "Buck, this is Sherry, Mary Ann's friend. Have you talked to her today?"

"Oh hi, Sherry. Sorry about the time and dime thing, I thought you were Russell wanting to bug me about my golf game today. About Mary Ann, I called just after my game today, but she didn't have time to talk; she was washing her hair or something. She was going to call me later but she hasn't." Buck paused a moment, then continued. "To tell you the truth, she sounded like she was mad at me, or something. It has me a little worried, to be honest. I thought we were getting along fine. Maybe I am golfing too much."

"Nah, Buck, I don't think so. Do me a favor and call her now. If you get her, ask her to call me. If you do not get her, please call me back at this number." After giving Buck the number, she hung up.

"I heard you tell Stella we might fly tonight. Do you think it is that serious?"

"Honey, you would never sleep here tonight, and we may as well be in the air." They were interrupted by the phone. It was Buck.

"Sherry, she has gone out of town. She must be mad because she did not tell me a thing, or call. Man, I hope I haven't messed this up. She is the nicest lady I have met since my wife passed a few years ago." It sounded sorta like Buck was crying.

"No Buck, I know Mary Ann is very fond of you. Does she have a friend with a black pickup or a black Hummer?"

"Huh uh, not that I know of, but I do not know all her friends. I have never heard of a Hummer being around there."

Jerry motioned he would like to talk. Sherry nodded. "Buck, my husband Jerry would like to talk a minute. Here he is."

"Buck, this is Jerry. I am looking forward to meeting you. You know how women are; Sherry is worried about Mary Ann. We are in Pittsburg now, but we will fly out just as soon as possible. How far do you live from Zack's Ford Road?"

"Hi Jerry, I sure want to meet you also. I live about twenty minutes from there."

"This may not be important, but I like to cover all bases. We would appreciate it if you could go to the trailer park, the one on the left just after you turn onto Zack's Ford Road. Drive up to lot number ten, knock and ask if Johnny Thomas has left a phone and is waiting for a reward? Do you have fifty dollars I could borrow?"

"Sure Jerry. Why?"

"Give the kid or his dad a fifty dollar reward. The kid found Mary Ann's phone on the side of the road. He answered when Sherry called."

"What was the phone doing on the side of the road?"

"Trust me to fill you in later. This is important. So, please do not ask any questions at the trailer. Right now the important thing is to get the phone. Take a baggie and as soon as you can, put it in the baggie. We may have to check for fingerprints. I may be overreacting and I certainly hope so, but until we know, let's preserve any leads or evidence we can."

"You mean go now and get the phone, don't you?" Short pause. "You are scaring me, Jerry. Do you think seriously that something bad has happened?"

"Yes, get the phone as soon as possible. And Buck, right now, you know about as much as we do. Let's play it by ear. One more question. There should be an airport around there with the furniture executives flying in and out. Do you know where it is?"

"Sure, it is on North Carolina 27, name is Lower Creek Airport. I play golf with Russell Kerfoot. He either owns or manages it."

"Great, most of those airports are landing with permission only. I'd appreciate it if you would call Russell and tell him we want to use his runway. And I will double his fees."

"You mean tonight? I don't think they have lights."

"How does the weather look outside down there?"

"Clear as a bell and nearly a full moon."

"No problem. My girl can do that, maybe using your help. Give Sherry your cell number. We will call when we are close." Pause. "And Buck, if there is a problem, someone will pay, but above all we must ensure Mary Ann's safety."

"Jerry, I think I would die if something happened to her; after this many years I hoped I had found the best wife in the world. I had to make myself wait to propose, and I haven't yet. Do you know what I mean?"

"Yeah Buck," he said, turned his head and met Sherry's eyes. "Yeah, I am sure I know EXACTLY what you mean. You get the phone and go to the airport and wait. Get you some snacks and coffee, you may need it. Oh, and one more thing, after the phone capture, you should have time to drive by Mary Ann's house. Do that, see if something is askew. Look in, but if it is locked, leave it as is. I will have a crew look for anything you cannot see. We do not want to disturb anything in that house until we know more."

"I am on my way, Jerry. Hurry on down."

Jerry called Stella to ready the craft as soon as possible. Of course, she said it was almost ready now. He should have known that girl would start immediately. He told her to look up Lower Creek Airport near Lenoir, NC. "That is where we will set down. Also plan the top speed of your bird. Get us a rental delivered to Lower Creek. The car can be left in the care of a gentleman named Buck who will be waiting."

Jerry walked back to the kitchen. He keyed the message machine and explained to Mama why they were not in the house and gave her his love as he signed off. She was just a little older than he was but she had always been like a mother to him.

Jerry hit speed dial for Tuck on his phone. "Yeah, what you want?" Came the answer, "I am busy watching the grass grow."

"I figured a famous person like you would be doing something very important, but I was wondering maybe if you could help me cut some grass."

"At present, I am all ears."

"Do you have any assets near Lenoir, NC?"

"No, but let me check with Buddy. I will get right back to you."

In less than two minutes, he had a return conference call. "Buddy is on line with us."

"Hey boss, Stephen, Reece and Jenn are appearing in Blowing Rock for some Appalachian State College dinner. They finished up about an hour ago. They are not on the clock; it was just one of their entertainment and musical gigs."

After giving the address, "I need Reece and Stephen inside that house ASAP. Lift fingerprints from knobs, phone, etc.—the usual. Mary Ann, who lives there, is missing. She went missing less than 4-5 hours ago. Make a clean job as usual. Jen can cover the outside as the look-see; she is good at sight detail."

"You need Tuck and me?"

"I want you available. Tell Stephen we will meet him at the Lower Creek Airport or at the house, depending on the time."

"Will do. We will get the details concerning Mary Ann when we meet up or later. I always liked that girl." Tuck said.

"Yeah, you would say that. He had a crush on her at one time boss." Buddy said.

"You guys take it easy. Like always, I hope we are barking up a wrong tree." They all signed off.

Jerry did not use a chauffeur anymore, so the car would stay at the airport awaiting their return.

Sherry only had to pack her favorite toiletries; there were always two complete changes of clothes hanging in the plane closet, and extra shoes. Stella had her own small closet that she shared with Vickie, if she flew.

The flight would take about an hour, with Stella adding the extra coal. They would probably fly at maximum speed which for the Lear is near 500mph. The flight was about that many miles.

It took about an hour to reach the airport. Stella was waiting with the flight plan filed. Vickie would be going on this trip because they did not know how long the plane would be away from Pittsburg. Within twenty minutes, Stella had them airborne.

Sherry sat beside her handsome husband. As she looked at Jerry Wiley, she could not help but thank God for allowing this match. Right now, she had no idea what the future held, but she knew with God's help, Jerry Wiley would handle whatever they faced. He was a miracle worker.

****

Meanwhile, down in a small area north of Hickory, NC, a man called Buck was secretly praying that the woman he loved was okay, and would eventually be his bride. Buck served as deacon at his church, always tried to be a good guy. But right now, he thought, if someone had harmed Mary Ann, they would answer to him.

He called his friend Russell and, after some wrangling about runway lights, Russell grudgingly said, "Okay, but Buck, this isn't like parking a car. I will head for the airport."

CHAPTER 2

THE MYSTERY

Buck's life had been uncomplicated. His had been a good marriage, with children and a forty hour week. The family had experienced the normal growing pains and problems. They had never wanted for much, but they had lived a simple life in the furniture producing capitol of the Carolinas. The loss of his wife had been devastating. To fill the void, he had taken up golf, but in his later life, the family support kept him going; he had been a good dad.

As he was trying to put his life back together, he grew closer to Mary Ann. Actually; he had known Mary Ann from afar because of the marriage of their grandchildren. But now, he had become romantically involved; something new to him. Their relationship stirred feelings he had forgotten he possessed. He had tried to let golf fill his life, but this was better by far.

He was still a man and a pretty woman like Mary Ann naturally caused some renewed, old feelings below in the furnace. He now smiled thinking about it as he drove up US 321 toward Lenoir. Then he got to thinking how she sounded over the phone. Using his cell phone, he called her again. He listened better this time, and this time she did not sound mad at him, just strange—a sound he had never heard in her voice. He turned off the highway, then on Zack's Ford Road. He went into the trailer park and easily found number 10. He smiled in relief when he saw plenty of lights in the trailer.

He approached the door and rang the bell. Footsteps approached. In moments, a young man appeared with a teenager by his side. "Can I help you?" he asked.

"Dr. Wiley called and said you had Mary Ann's phone here. She asked me to retrieve it, and give the young man a reward for finding it."

"I found it. It is banged up but it still works. Here it is," the boy spoke anxiously.

Buck took the phone in a light grip. "Thank you, son, Mary Ann will be very glad to get this back." Handing the young dad a Ziploc bag, he added, "Here is your son's reward. Let him open it and count it." The man took the bag, looked at it, and handed it to his son. After counting the money, the boy's eyes opened wide and a smile crossed his face. Buck casually reached out for the zip lock bag and the boy gave it to him.

"I guess it ain't important, but why ain't the owner picking it up?" asked the man.

"Good question," said Buck. "She is out of town and may not even know the phone is missing. The doctor was trying to call her when Johnny here answered. The doctor and Mary Ann are good friends; she is not a patient, just a friend, so she's doing her a favor. You may not know it, but you were talking to the doctor in Pittsburg. She called me in Hickory because Mary Ann is my girlfriend."

Johnny laughed a little at that.

"Aw Johnny, us old boys got girlfriends, too!" They all laughed.

Buck thanked them and while walking back to his pickup, he dropped the phone into another baggie he had in his coat pocket.

Once in his truck, Buck drove the familiar roads to Mary Ann's house. Her van was still in the drive way, and there was one light on in the living room. Parking his truck, he left it running with the door open, and walked up on the porch. He smiled at the flowers on the railing that Mary Ann loved and cared for so patiently. He knocked on the door, at first lightly, then heavily, with no response. The living room curtains were open and he could see directly inside; nothing seemed out of place. Buck had watched enough TV to know he did not want to mess up any fingerprints, so he lightly checked the knob to see if it was locked. It was. He then walked around the house, but nothing looked out of place. Now his mind was going wild—the van here, no answer, the lost cell phone, and a strange message about going out of town. Being a fairly religious man, Buck breathed a prayer. *God, I love this woman. Please let everything be all right. As always, this is Buck.*

Back to his truck, he headed toward the airport, anxious to learn anything he could about his new girlfriend. As he arrived at the Lower Creek Airport he saw the lights on in the office and Russell's car already there. As he pulled in, he was followed by two cars from a rental company in Hickory.

The lead driver walked over to where Russell had just come out to meet Buck. "Is one of you guys Buck? I don't have a last name on the bill."

"That's me, what do you need?"

"Nothing, I am bringing a car for a Jerry Wiley. He must be somebody; the bosses don't send us out like this for Joe Blow. Here are the keys. My instructions were to leave them with you."

"Do I owe you anything?" Buck asked.

"Nada, Mr. Wiley more than took care of the bill and tip. By the way, tell him thanks and give us a call anytime."

"Will do."

As the rental folks left, Russell asked, "What is this all about, Buck? I didn't know you had flying friends. You never mentioned it."

Buck took Russell through what he knew and they waited, just passing the time and talking about the possibilities of Mary Ann's disappearance and a little golf. Then Buck's cell phone rang.

"Hello, this is Buck."

"Hi Buck, this is Stella, pilot for Jerry Wiley, I should be seeing you in five minutes. I need to verify a couple things about the runway." Buck handed the phone to Russell.

"This is Russell Kerfoot. How can I help you?"

"This is Lear Jet 60, Stella the pilot. Are you still Turf with a length of four K feet?"

"Lear Jet 60, your stats are correct. I am afraid I cannot give permission. We are a little short of your requirements, Morganton fits you better."

"I am sure you are right, Mr. Kerfoot, but I am about to show a red light on fuel and need to set her down. Four thousand feet is good."

"Are you declaring an emergency?"

"You could say that. I see you now. I want to make a low pass first. It is very clear tonight and this is beautiful country."

"I repeat, Morganton fits you best. I have ears here. I am on record with that statement."

"I understand, Mr. Kerfoot. My boss will take full responsibility, and you can put that on record also." With that transmission, the Lear Jet 60 dropped to about three hundred feet on a pass then climbed back to one thousand feet. "I need only one thing. I would like for Buck to drive that big pickup to the end of the runway, with his emergency flashers on, and stop at the very end. I will land in four minutes."

Buck had heard Stella and looked at Russell, who nodded and indicated to 'get going'. Running to his truck, he headed down the runway with his flashers on. As he reached the end of the runway, looking in his rear view mirror, he could see the plane coming in with its bright landing lights beaming.

****

Inside the plane, everyone was buckled in and ready for a rough landing. Just over the office, Stella cut power and the plane dropped like lead to within twenty-five feet of the runway, when she gave it full power and full flaps for one second before pulling back. As she pulled back, the wheels touched down; she let it run for five or six hundred feet, and dropped the engine's power. They rolled within a hundred feet of the pick-up and Stella did a 180 and taxied back to the office with Buck following.

Stella spotted the apron parking and pulled in, then cut power. "Welcome to Lower Creek Airport in Lenoir, temp sixty seven degrees with no wind and clear skies. Thank you for flying Wiley Industries Airlines." They all breathed a sigh of relief and unbuckled. The door swung open and they alighted in Lenoir.

Russell and Buck met them. Introducing themselves, they shook hands. Russell sought out Stella. "I want to shake your hand, pilot. That was some landing."

"I'll do better than that," she said, reaching up to hug him and kiss him on the cheek, "You have a great set up here with some fantastic landing lights." She pointed to the full moon. "Buck, the tail lights did help."

After a few minutes, Russell invited them inside where they could sit and talk comfortably. "I put some coffee on; it is about ready. I do this often. I drink coffee anytime."

"We all may share it," Jerry said. "I am not sure how long we will be up. I know we will probably drive to Mt. Bell tonight."

"What?" asked Stella in mock surprise. "You leave me with Buck and Russell? You don't trust me to take off in these mountains at night? That really hurts, boss." Everyone got a good laugh that was needed to relieve some tension.

The conversation turned serious with Sherry and Jerry reciting what they knew. Buck told them about the phone retrieval and his swing by the house. Jerry told everyone that he had his own forensic crew that should be at Mary Ann's house now. Russell raised his eyebrows and Buck showed surprise.

"You what? Already? That is impossible," he blurted.

"Actually, it is luck; the crew was in Blowing Rock when I called a couple hours ago. They only had to come down the mountain to Mary Ann's house." Giving that time to sink in, he continued, "If they are not here in the next fifteen minutes, we will go back to Greening Heights and Mary Ann's house."

"Should we notify the police?" asked Buck, puzzled at the speed everything was happening.

"Buck, let's wait a little while. I doubt if the sheriff or the local police department are ready for this. That is if it is what it looks like on the surface. But believe me I have been in the investigating business for many years. Not everything is as it appears. Just as there are many reasons this could be bad, there are just as many for it being something simple. It could be as simple as her son Dusty just bought a Hummer and he is taking her for a ride. We will check with her family after we have the cursory look inside her house."

"Yeah, I know you are probably right, Jerry. I have heard rumors about you, and I know you are not here just for a quick plane ride to land on a grass runway with no lights at night. No offense, Russell."

They chatted about the things that appeared strange. About Mary Ann's cell phone, for instance—did she throw it out or was it dropped? Russell mentioned that he had once bought an expensive flashlight to use at the airport. He had left it on this truck bumper to go back in the store, then when he came out, he drove off forgetting all about the flashlight and it fell off somewhere on his way from the hardware store to here. He never found it. Mary Ann could have done the same with her phone. In a few minutes, a dark minivan pulled in behind the other cars.

Stephen, Jennifer and Reece disembarked and came over. Reece took out a note pad as everyone was introduced. "Reece made some notes while we were in the house and some on the way down. She will give you what we have and then Jen and I will give additions if necessary. Go Reece."

"Hi everybody, we had just finished the gig and the van was packed when we got the call so we made it pretty quick. First, the house was easy to enter after Stephen stuck the knob to save any prints. Of course, we knocked and called with no answer. We stuck the phone and inside knobs and…"

"When Reece says stuck, she is saying the prints were lifted by clear cellophane tape," Jerry interrupted. "Sorry Reece, continue."

"There was no sign of a scuffle or any type of violence. Nothing out of place, the house was clean as usual with Mary Ann. I have visited before with Sherry. That made this sweep fairly simple. The only mysterious thing was a crumpled note in the trash can. We took a picture and put it back in the can. We could not lift prints, but you wanted a clean entry. Of course we can go get it if you want. Another thing was a couple phone calls coming in with no messages, in reality not unusual. We noted the knife drawer in the kitchen was not closed completely and there was an empty slot for an eight inch butcher knife." Hearing that, Buck made a noise.

"Buck?" Sherry asked.

"That knife is at my house. The handle was loose and Mary Ann asked me to tighten it."

"One less thing to be concerned about. Thanks, Buck."

Jen held up a finger and pointed to Stephen. "Casts?"

"Oh yeah, going in I poured a quick setting mix to make a cast of the four big tires. That is why we were a little late; they are set and in the van. I could see two footprints and got those also. I did not disturb the earth too much."

"Anything to add?" Jerry asked.

Reece looked down at the pad. "Programmable thermostat has these settings: 'Normal Activities', 'off and on', 'Away Summer', and 'Away winter'. The 'Normal Activities' setting was active."

"Uh," Buck started and cleared his throat. "We haven't left her house on dates but a few times, yet every time we did she went to that thermostat, and explained she ALWAYS hit the away button when she left."

"Add that to the notes, Stephen," Jerry said.

"Done, there were no windows or doors opened, no sign of forced entry. The phone was square on the table, all neat as if the owner had stepped out on the porch." Stephen closed the notebook.

Everyone stood around trying to digest what information was available. After a minute, Jerry spoke, "Sherry, you should call her children and ask if their mama is with them. If she isn't, just see what you can find out. I suggest calling the son who is in law enforcement first."

Sherry stepped outside to get a better signal for the cell. The rest stayed inside, drinking Russell's coffee and trying to piece together something that made sense, but nothing seemed to work with the available information. Jennifer did suggest it might be a good idea to have someone look at her computer, maybe even dump it if and before law enforcement impounded it. Stephen made a note to call Josh, the computer geek in the group.

Jerry gave Russell and Buck a Reader's Digest version of what he and his crew did in the past. He wanted to allay any feelings that he was interfering in law enforcement. "With what we have here, the police will not post a missing person's alert for three days, much less start an investigation."

Sherry came into the room. She had talked to Debbie, Robyn and Dusty. "No one knows of any plans their mother had to go out of town. The girls want us to keep in touch. They both are praying, of course. Dusty has no idea who might have a Hummer that his mama knows. The family has plans for tomorrow night, celebrating her oldest granddaughter's birthday. He said his mother would not miss that for the world, and I agree. He also said for sure she had not said anything about leaving town. He is going to request a day off and be on his way to his mom's house. I asked him to be careful, reminding him it concerns his mom and it might be a crime scene. He agreed, but he said he had to do something. The girls are going to call everyone they knew, to see if anyone had any idea about their mother's whereabouts."

"Russell, I hate to impose, but can we hang around a little while longer. We will gladly reimburse you for your time," Jerry addressed Russell.

"Hey, that's no problem, Jerry. If Buck is involved, I hate to see a guy's golf score ruined due to stress, so if it will help of course take all the time you want. If need be, I will let you lock up."

With that, Jerry took his cell phone and started calling. "Tuck, I need Matt to call this number," he said, giving Mary Ann's number. "Have him record the message and analyze it. If he needs Luke, put him on the clock also; this may require some time if you guys can spare it. I will let you know in the next few hours or tomorrow. Hang in there, dude."

He then called Buddy and gave him a run down. Of course, Buddy said, "My time is yours. I know it is the same with Leon and Sticky. Just call."

Jerry hung up. "Can anyone think of anything else?" he asked, looking around.

"Once we know that we cannot locate Mary Ann, we need to have Josh and his new partner in crime,

Megan, look into any security cameras that might cover any of these roads. That needs to be done within seventy-two hours or they start recording over the history," Stephen said.

"Good point, more?"

"What about cameras at airports and departing flights?" Jen said.

"Hummer rentals?" Sherry added, as she saw that Reece was now writing all suggestions in the notepad.

"You know what? We really need prints from the boy and his dad, the ones that found that phone, so Matt and Luke can disregard them."

"I was hoping I had done something right. Here is a baggie with both prints on it. I watch Police TV a lot and I thought of that." Grinning, Buck handed him a baggie with another baggie inside.

"Buck, dude, you are a marvel. If I were starting over you would be hired." Everyone laughed and Buck had a satisfied, proud grin still on his face at the compliment.

As time came to break up, Stephen and his party

headed to Charlotte. Jen had work the next day. Jerry suggested Buck might want to get some sleep, but there was no way he was going to relax. Stella and Vickie were dropped off at a motel. At the same time, Jerry reserved a couple of rooms for them and Buck and Dusty. Then, Sherry, Jerry and Buck headed for Mary Ann's house to wait for Dusty to arrive.

CHAPTER 3

IMPACT – SHE IS MISSING

The community Mary Ann lived in was called Greening Heights, Lenoir's premium retirement and Recreation Vehicle Resort. In the evenings, the gate is controlled by a password changed weekly. Leaving Greening Heights, the gate opens automatically by sensors as a vehicle approaches. The place has been a 'No Crime' area for years. No one has felt the need for surveillance cameras and residents have always felt completely safe.

Entering Greening Heights earlier, Stephen used a random number generator that instantly finds the simple four digit number of any code. He and Josh had developed this on MVA events years before. With approval, Greening Heights had issued Buck and Mary Ann's family an override number that never changed. It was created especially for permanent residents and their guests.

Buck had given Jerry the code and they all were now at the top of the mountain at Mary Ann's house waiting. They dared not enter the house and stayed a good twenty-five yards away to preserve any evidence they might find when daylight arrived. They were also hoping that by morning there would be a simple explanation for a missing Mary Ann, and they could all get a good laugh.

But Sherry was already sure something was awry. "Mary Ann loves this place. When I expressed fears of her living alone here, she would always laugh. That girl could put you at ease with that laugh. She felt very safe high above the rest of Greening Heights. Having a gated community seems to give that safe feeling."

Jerry agreed that something seemed to be wrong, but outwardly he did not want to seem too concerned. Buck, on the other hand, was willing to agree with Sherry; he was getting anxious. "I hope Dusty gets here soon. Mary Ann is very proud of him being a law enforcement officer. Maybe he can look around and find an answer. Lord, I hope so."

Being on top of the mountain, sounds carry very well at night. Everyone heard the siren in the distance. It was probably as far away as US 321 coming into Lenoir. Jerry guessed in his mind that a son being concerned about his mother could get the okay to use the siren in route to check on his mother. There is an unwritten rule of supporting your fellow LEO (law enforcement officer). The sound became louder and it was obvious it had reached Zack's Ford Road, and then the siren went silent. Ten minutes later a County Mountie car arrived, of course it was Dusty, still in uniform.

He hugged Sherry and greeted everyone. "Okay, what is happening?"

Jerry briefed Dusty about all they knew, plus what his crew had done and was doing; and that the phone was on its way to a lab to be examined. His mother's voice was being professionally analyzed and by all indications, something was not right about her not being seated comfortably here at her home at this hour.

Dusty had a key to his mom's house. "I think I would like to go inside myself and look around." It was not a question. "I will not disturb anything; I just need to see for myself."

"Of course, I know I would feel the same. Please leave the only piece of paper in the small trash can as it is for local law enforcement or the FBI. I have a photocopy you can read later." Jerry put emphasis on the FBI. "The feds may be able to get prints off the paper. You know, if she in fact has been kidnapped, it would be a federal offense."

"I understand that. I will be back out shortly," Dusty said as he left the group, carefully made his way to the door, and disappeared inside. Jerry knew there was a possibility Dusty, knowing his mom and also being a LEO, might spot something Stephen's crew had overlooked. They talked among themselves while awaiting some—they hoped— good news. "It is good Dusty is a LEO. He knows not to disrupt a possible crime scene. And besides, he could come up with something good," Jerry commented.

In just a few minutes, Dusty came out. "Jerry, something is wrong here. Mama has always pointed out to anyone coming into her house, 'This is my kids in order of their age,' and she would name us. From the time this house was built, our three photos have been in the same order on that mantle. Now, I am shown as the oldest plus the frames are not straight. Mom always kept them neatly lined up. I have never been first."

"So what are you saying, Dusty?"

"I am going down to Lenoir to report Mama missing. They may not do anything, but I am going to insist at least they mark this as a crime scene. Until they or we know more. The most they can do is waste a roll of CRIME SCENE tape."

"My thinking exactly son, I like that. We have a room for you and Buck at the motel near the sports complex. We will also be spending the night at the same motel and I will start the ball rolling with our investigation team. Sherry thinks the world of your mom and we will do anything we can to ensure her safe return, if the worst we fear has happened. However, I am hoping some dude or dudess from her past has shown up in a Hummer and they have just gone for some crazy drive."

"I'd drink to that. I am off. Thanks for your cell numbers. You know mine. Call if anything, I mean *anything*, comes up. I will do the same." Dusty shook hands and hugged Sherry, and then took off down the mountain.

"Buck, I think we are all tired and should hit the

sack. Call in the morning or we will call you if you would like to have breakfast. Maybe we will talk to the local law. I will do what I can over the phone tonight." They said good night and headed down the mountain. They finally agreed on breakfast the next morning at the sports center at nine AM. It was quiet in the rental as they headed to the motel. Jerry could not help but think of the excitement of having the MVA crew together again.

Jerry had nurtured and supported the four boys who had harassed him during his time as a street person; the same boys that had tagged him 'Rags'. A bond had been formed. Sticky, Tuck, Buddy and J. Leon had become men with integrity. Through all the MVA events, some including facing deadly force, they had stuck together like glue. After the MVA was disbanded, they had all set up companies of their own. Sticky had stayed with his first love, heavy equipment and road construction. The other three had formed investigative services businesses. J. Leon leaned toward the technical side of things; he even had satellites at his command. Buddy and Tuck were known worldwide for their successes. BUT, the MVA had been where it all started. They subcontracted to the CIA and FBI, teaching Survival and Terrorist Control. Jerry could not help but smile, even in the face of this disaster.

"I see that smile," Sherry said. "You are thinking how good it would be to have the crew back together, I know."

"Guilty as charged. You are so danged insightful, it is scary, sweetheart."

"Well, let me tell you, if this is anything like I am afraid it is, this is one woman who is glad she married the miracle worker, Jerry Wiley."

As they pulled up to the motel, Jerry said, "Well, let's hope in the morning Mary Ann has called the Lenoir Police Department or Caldwell County Sheriff to ask what crime was committed at her house."

"I agree with that, sweetheart."

Chapter 4

MORNING IN THE MOUNTAINS

The morning came with bright sunshine in the North Carolina Mountains. Dusty informed Jerry that the sheriff had taped Mary Ann's house, but they would do nothing for three days, the normal missing person's rule, unless violence could be proven or was obvious.

Jerry, Sherry, Dusty and Buck were sitting at a table discussing the situation when the phone rang. "Okay, where are you Sherlock?" Buddy said from the other end of the line. "The Calvary is arriving in Lenoir on US-321. It is tough keeping Tuck and Leon awake, something silly about flying all night to get here."

"We didn't expect you so soon my friend, but continue on North on 321 until you see the Sports Complex on the left. We are at the café. Welcome aboard." Smiling broadly, he hung up.

"So your boys couldn't wait to get back into harness as the MVA, huh?" Sherry said as the breakfast arrived at their table.

"I don't think Sticky is with them, but yes, Buddy, Tuck and J. Leon are here. And of course I am glad to know my adopted sons are here. No one could ask for better help."

Before they were half through with breakfast, the

riot arrived. They were noisy and fired up, giving hugs all around, followed by introductions. The waitress arrived with the breakfast that Jerry had ordered for the three. "I guess marriage hasn't completely ruined you, boss. The breakfast is perfect." J. Leon grinned.

"It is pretty hard to forget eggs sunny side up, grits, ham and pancakes along with strong coffee." Sherry laughed.

As they ate, Tuck said, "Analyzing the phone message, Matt would only say Mary Ann was under stress when she recorded the message. Luke's opinion was someone was beside her and she seemed to be *reading*, rather than *saying*." Tuck paused briefly to chew on his food. "Something about the ending—normally there is a little time, maybe three to four seconds when a person recording a message pauses at the end. This one was ended abruptly, like a second party had hung up the phone."

"This is just what we were afraid of," Jerry said with a sigh, "We need some ideas, and here is what we know." Jerry recited from his notes what they had so far. Things were being batted around. The three guys just arriving were going to check for locations of security cameras in the area. Of course, they were hoping to get a Hummer pickup tag number. J. Leon wanted to talk to the kid again to see if he could remember *anything* more about the Hummer. In all the excitement around the table, Buck's phone rang.

"Sure Russell, we are in the café at the Sports Complex." Pause… "You bet, we would love to talk to him. Bring him on in for coffee and donuts or breakfast, my treat."

"What is it, Buck?" Jerry asked.

"When Russell went to work this morning, his neighbor stopped by for coffee as usual. He said something that Russell thought we would be interested in. Jerry, yours was not the only plane that landed at Lower Creek Airport last night. The one before you did not have permission to land and take off. The kicker is that a big black pickup met the plane."

The table all of a sudden got quiet. Everyone's mind was shifting gear to take in the new information. In about ten minutes, Russell came in with a small bearded guy. "Fellows, this is Melvin

Peace. He lives across from Lower Creek Airport. I will let him tell you what he told me this morning." Before Melvin started, Jerry introduced everyone all round then thanked Melvin for coming over to talk.

"Shucks, it ain't no big deal. I am always out and about at all hours. Early evening 'bout seb'n a'clock, I see'd this big black pickup truck, four doors 'n all, turn in t'Lower Creek. I thought he was turnin' around, but he drove on down to the end of the runway and sat with his parking lights on. Afore I thought too long a plane swooped in, one of 'em lil two motor jobs, you know; looked mostly white with some black stripes down the side. Wings wuz bent up on the ends. I ain't never figured that out. Anyway, he landed and met up with the big pickup. Two folks, a tall woman and a small man with a red hat on backwards got out of the back seat and climbed into the plane. I could tell the lady had sorta shiny hair, white, blonde or grey, y'know. At's about it, 'cept the plane swung around and took off torge me with the pickup sorta following it like it was pushing it; at made me smile cause I 'ad never seen nothing like at."

"Melvin, I think the law folk will probably want to talk to you later, do you mind that?"

"Nah, I know all 'em boys. I will be glad to tell it agin." Melvin was peppered with questions and seemed to enjoy the attention. He had given them a lot of information, much they really did not want to hear. They were all convinced now that Mary Ann had been abducted, but the reason was missing.

"Mel, didn't you say you got some numbers?" asked Russell.

"Oh yeah, 'at sucker went right over my head when he taken off. Just over me, he leaned torge town and I see'd the number on its tail, N dash 198 something. They wuz one or two more numbers or letters, I did'n make 'em. And then the big black pickup turned this way, back torge town ye know."

They all talked awhile and as Russell and Mel were leaving, Jerry slipped Mel a hundred dollar bill, and Mel smiled ear to ear.

"I think it is time to do some serious investigating." Three laptops were already out and clicking as Jerry said that. "You guys have my number. I am going downtown to talk to the local law enforcement about what we just learned. Now we are pretty sure Mary Ann was put on that plane. Question is, why and by whom?" Jerry took in

Buck's expression. He was white as a sheet. "Hey Buck, how about you and Dusty talking over what we just learned? Sherry and I will head to the local law house. Also, if you don't mind, your knowledge of the area may help these guys as they start playing detective. Hang with them."

Buck only nodded.

Sherry and Jerry headed to downtown Lenoir. At the police station, Jerry introduced himself and let the man on the desk know they were there because they had information concerning a crime that had possibly been committed. Chief Brown came out to speak to them in person. "Mr. Wiley, Officer Dusty said you might be in. Unfortunately, we can't help. Greening Heights is out of our jurisdiction. Our duty man made a log entry and referred him to the County Sheriff, Sheriff Jones."

Jerry and Chief Brown had a short talk, and his countenance turned a little when Lower Creek Airport was mentioned—that was in his jurisdiction, "Dusty did not know about the airport being used to *possibly* being used to remove his mom from this area. We just learned that from Melvin Peace."

"Melvin is sort of a local character. He is a good fellow, but he does embellish a lot."

"I am a pretty good judge of character, Chief, and I got the same feeling; however, the events he described over coffee with Russell, without any hint of a problem existing, are completely believable."

"Mr. Wiley, give me a minute. I will check if the Sheriff has time for a meeting." With Jerry's nod, the Chief walked over to a desk. Jerry and Sherry were still standing. The chief was gone only a few moments. "The sheriff just posted his troops and has time for a chat." After getting directions, the couple took off.

As they approached the entrance to the Sheriff's office, the door opened. "Dr. Wiley, Sheriff Jones here. You know the Internet is a wonderful tool. It doesn't take long to research some names. What in the world are you doing up in our neck of the woods, so far from Pittsburg and Duke University, I might add?"

"Hello Sheriff, I'm flattered. This is my wife, Dr. Sherry Wiley. The reason isn't so mysterious. My wife called her friend and she sounded strange on the phone. I trust her intuition so much; we flew down and landed at Lower Creek Airport to check on her friend."

"Yes, I understand from notes in the log that Officer Dusty, her son, asked for her home to be listed as a crime scene. Believe it or not, my man on duty believed the young man, called me, and I did authorize that. I know he, and probably you, understand we cannot take any official action for three days, unless violence or a crime have obviously been committed."

"I want to be honest upfront, Sheriff. I have close connections with the FBI and CIA." Seeing the defensive face on the sheriff, Jerry smiled, "Whoa, don't take that statement wrong. This is no power play. I just want you to understand that this is not my first rodeo; I was once in the CIA. Later, I formed a corporation with some of the best investigators in the world and have worked closely with many law enforcement communities. I knew no one would be able to act until something was a fact. So with Dusty's approval, I have called my top men in. The phone message has already been analyzed." Jerry paused as the sheriff's countenance changed to a more cooperative look, "I have three of the best, most experienced men in the world right now at the sports complex, following up on what we just learned. I have one man who owns satellites, and can move them to assist. We will gladly share any investigative information and if you would like, we will be of any assistance we possibly can to your office. At this time, as a man who has investigated hundreds of crimes of this nature, I am telling you that my wife's good friend Mary Ann has been kidnapped from her home atop Greening Heights, and she was flown out of Lower Creek Airport not long before my plane landed at that same field."

Showing his professional side, the sheriff spoke, "I have a few contacts with the FBI myself, Dr. Wiley, and of course I will check out your credentials. Those things aside, come on into my office. I do have at least thirty minutes. Let's talk." As they walked by the front desk, he stopped to scribble a note, handed it to the deputy and said, "Tom, get me Bill Muse on the phone."

Inside the office, the sheriff offered and served hot black coffee.

"Sheriff, I don't think you will learn too much from Bill, down in Mt. Holly."

"Why is that, Dr. Wiley?"

"First of all, please call me Jerry. I feel more comfortable. Now to Agent Muse, as FBI, he was assigned to work with a CIA Agent named Sam Colson. The job was to find and detain me. I was AWOL from the CIA, and the agency was afraid I was going to embarrass them. I had no intention of being detained or of embarrassing the Agency. That was early in Bill's career; he was working with an agent he did not care for. Long story short, Colson turned out to be a rogue, and was killed accidentally by his own son, Silas. Later, Bill assisted my men in locating Silas, who was at the time a kidnapper. Bill passed away a few months back, and I hated to see it. We were friends." There was a knock on the door and the deputy stepped in and handed the sheriff a note.

The sheriff held the note and studied it for a moment. "Seems his wife Brenda says he passed away. When your name was mentioned, she said that Bill trusted you as much as anyone he had met. Pretty good recommendation, I'd say." The sheriff relaxed visibly. "So Jerry, what do you know? Let's get this underway."

After an hour's discussions, the sheriff learned that Sherry had also been a victim of kidnapping and knows a kidnapping situation up close and personal. She therefore fears for Mary Ann's life. The circumstantial evidence was there, and the sheriff was convinced that it was a kidnapping. He followed protocol and contacted the FBI office in Raleigh earlier to give them a head's up on what was very possibly happening.

As Jerry and Sherry were leaving to head back to the sports complex, he commented to the sheriff, "By now the boys should have a written copy of the voice analysis and maybe a lead on the plane. You have my number; we will be in touch. And thank you, Sheriff; it is always a pleasure to work with a professional."

Back in the car, they settled for the ride. "I am sure the sheriff is going to do some digging into our lives first and then look at the kidnapping. I think he is a good guy."

"I agree sweetheart, but I am going crazy trying to figure and reason this out. I cannot help but wonder what is going through Mary Ann's mind. I knew you would be working on my behalf when I was at the mercy of Colson, but she cannot know we—you—are on this one now. Oh, by the way, thinking of investigating, Buddy said he had some more stuff in the van and would need a place to set up."

"Good thinking. Sweetie, let's see what the motel has on the way back."

CHAPTER 5

THE SHERIFF IS ONBOARD

Within the hour, Sheriff Jones had his top investigator in his office. After giving him a quick but thorough summary of the situation, and three names to research, Drs. Jerry and Sherry Wiley and Mary Ann Kirkman, he was ready to get the ball rolling. "Find out what you can on the net. I will call the North Carolina Office of the FBI to see what they have."

Deputy Billy Rankin nodded. "I will get right on it, Sheriff. From what I hear you say, you are on a fence with this. Of course, you know we really do not have the equipment needed or budget to follow this too far. I am curious to know who these 'experts' are that Dr. Wiley has already on site. That is mighty fast for something that happened last evening."

"Correct you are, Rankin, but I know the man is very wealthy, and money can do a lot of things."

"You got that right; I will get back to you as soon as I get something." Deputy Rankin headed for his office.

Before making his calls, the Sheriff sat pondering what they'd found out so far. 'We never have been power hungry here in the mountains, but if this thing is of interest to the famous Dr. Jerry Wiley, it may get a lot of coverage. That could lead to a larger budget over time and get us some of the equipment we need.' With purpose, he picked up the phone, fluffed his rolodex to FBI, and dialed.

After going through the secretary, he was connected to the agent on duty. "Officer Beatty here, how may I help you, Sheriff?"

"Good morning, sir. I notified your office with a heads-up on a possible kidnapping here in the Lenoir area just a little while ago. But since then I have learned a few things. Dr. Jerry Wiley flew into the area last night to check on the lady suspected of being kidnapped. He just left my office. According to him, he has worked with the FBI at times on investigations. I am calling to see if anyone could verify that?"

"Well Sheriff, that story is used a lot. We do have many folk who work with us; many subcontractors, you might say," as Officer Beatty was talking, the sheriff heard the sound of a keyboard. He was probably searching for Dr. Wiley in the database. At one point, the typing stopped, and the silence stretched between them, a tad too long. "I have heard the name," Beatty finally said, "but I am afraid I cannot help you much, Sheriff. He was probably long before my time. But about this kidnapping, how long has it been?"

"From what I gather, it was late yesterday afternoon when Dr. Wiley's wife was talking to the missing lady and said her friend sounded strange. She called back just a little later and got the answering machine with a message saying she was going out of town and would return calls when she got back. Now I also understand the Wiley's were at their home in Pittsburg when she made those calls. She was so concerned they flew down in the doctor's plane and arrived here early last night."

"Seems awfully concerned, the ladies just being friends and all, wouldn't you say, Sheriff?"

"Yep, and not only that, Wiley says the answering machine message has already been analyzed by his experts, and he also has three of his top men here in Lenoir as of an hour ago."

"I tell you what, Sheriff, just to humor the doctor, and please do not repeat that, I will have a couple agents drop by this afternoon. It was wise of you to call, Sheriff. I will be in touch."

"Thanks from this end. Looking forward to working with your office if there is a case."

The sheriff put the phone in the cradle and smiled. *Beatty, I ain't the dumb mountain hick you think I am. There is something to Wiley or your office would not budge for three days, then I would have to pull teeth to get some help.* He widened the smile to a grin. *He did say a couple agents, and as of now there is only talk and some speculation. Yeah right, Agent in Charge Beatty.*

"Sheriff?" His thoughts were interrupted by Deputy Rankin. "I need to run some stuff by you."

"Leave the horns on it and run it by, Rankin."

"Mary Ann Kirkman is your average retiree. No convictions, not even a traffic citation. She has three children, two girls and a son who works for Gaston Rurals. She is retired from Textiles. She and her husband got in on the early years of Greening Heights, and lived there for years. He passed away a few years back. If she is kidnapped, it isn't for money."

"Jerry Wiley is quite different. He was a brain in the medical field, and rocketed to the top slot at Duke Medical. He never married and spent seven days a week in his office, never took a vacation. Under his leadership, new innovations took place and Duke claimed even more worldwide recognition. Then, just as suddenly, he resigned. NOTHING is known of his activities until he showed up as a bum in Mt. Bell, NC. That would never have been known if he had not saved a kid's life with his medical expertise. Next up, he became CEO of the family business in Pittsburg. Here it gets even stranger. He delegated the running of the business to an attorney, Fletcher, and set up a nonprofit organization listed as MVA. No meaning for the initials was ever given. What they do is unclear—things like 'assisting humanity', but their financial records go into the millions."

"Rankin, how the heck do you know all this in twenty to twenty-five minutes?"

"Sheriff, that ain't all. A couple…"

"I asked how you know all this."

Rankin looked a little embarrassed. "Wikipedia, Sheriff." Smiling, he continued. "What I just told you I retrieved in three minutes, but the strangest part I got from a computer file of newspaper articles. I found many of them about his wife, Dr. Sherry Oxnard Wiley, of the 'Oxnard Medical Clinic' down in Huntersville, NC."

"Oh yes, I remember that, a doctor was killed. He had been involved heavily in drugs if I remember right."

"Roger that, Sheriff, good memory. The doctor and an assistant were killed. Dr. Sherry Oxnard was cleared of all wrongdoing by a Grand Jury and the homicides were never solved."

"How did the two doctors become a pair with him in Pittsburg and her in Huntersville?"

"Newspaper article announcing the marriage says they attended Duke University together. They knew each other but were never romantically involved. Then we found another unrelated story, an interview with Doctor Jerry about the time he was a street person called 'Rags'. During the interview, he pointed out that later in Pittsburg, he read of Sherry's predicament in the newspaper and offered what help he could provide in the area of attorneys. She declined his offer, but they started corresponding."

"A real love story, huh?"

"Seems so. The last thing I have is more interesting since we are talking kidnapping here. On their honeymoon, at a stop in the little country of Belize, Sherry was kidnapped by a Silas Colson. During an altercation, she actually grabbed the controls and caused the plane to crash on takeoff. Colson was killed; she saved herself."

"Interesting folk, these Wileys, huh, Deputy?" he

said, following that with a pause.

"Colson, huh? Then, while you are looking at your Wikipedia, find out if this Colson or his family were ever attached to law enforcement."

"Yes, sir, I can do that. Now, after reading about the man Jerry Wiley, I want to get to know him," the deputy said.

"Then my good man, you should just do that very thing. Why don't you head on up to the sports complex north of town and introduce your own self? Give my regards to all and inform them that our trusty FBI says they might send an agent or two this afternoon."

"This afternoon? Wow, they usually don't even return calls. You evidently have developed quite a name, Sheriff, and Caldwell County finally got some pull, all right!"

"Get your butt out of here, Rankin, and solve this mystery for me."

"You got it. Shazam, I'm on my way."

As Rankin left his office, the Sheriff smiled and shook his head. "I hope we do not have a circus starting here," he said aloud to an empty room.

****

Beatty stared at the screen. He'd left the results up long after he entered Jerry Wiley's name into his system. Beside the name was a Black flag and a notation: 'NEED TO KNOW ONLY. SECRET CLEARANCE ALONG WITH SPECIAL PERMISSION REQUIRED'.

With a sigh, he exited the search screen, logged off the system, and resumed his scheduled tasks, hoping to make it home by dinner time.

CHAPTER 6

"JOINING FORCES, SORT OF"

Stopping at the motel, Jerry and Sherry selected the suite with a little kitchenette and bedroom with twin beds for their command center. The couch was a hide-a-bed, and the room was spacious. They paid for a week with a possible month's extension. They also kept the four rooms they already had, which included rooms for Vickie and Stella. The manager was very pleased; 'off seasons' are tough in the motel business. Now it was past the prime fall foliage season that drew the folks from the flat lands to this area. The cool months in the North Carolina Mountains lay ahead, and traffic died.

"Jerry, I think I know the answer to what I am going to ask, but I want to hear it: you will keep me in the loop, no matter how bad it may sound, won't you?"

"Yes, darling, that was always one of the principles on which my life and the MVA have been established. The truth will come out It is better that it is not a surprise to any of the active participants. You can never predict how folks will react. So yes, you have become my right-hand man, and I thank God you are a woman." He smiled over at her. "Never worry dear, we are one; you will know what I know."

At the sports complex, some locals were gathering in one noisy little corner. Sherry and Jerry recognized the local seniors who had chosen this place for their confabs. Every town has several places where the seniors meet up, so this was one. It is usually a happy corner with a lot of shared memories and laughing. Sherry thought, *Mary Ann cannot gather with her friends now*, as she felt tears forming.

They could easily see the crew was still hard at work; some were talking as the computers did whatever computers do while the operator is watching a blank screen. J. Leon seemed to have befriended Buck and they were both looking at his screen.

Tuck spotted the couple first. "Hey, boss," he called out, and motioned for them to come closer. He handed them several sheets of paper. "This is the complete voice analysis of Mary Ann's voice when she recorded the answering machine message. As you can see, it is straightforward. There are notes showing when she is 'most likely' not telling the truth, under pressure, and so on. The summary is by both Matt and Luke. On the surface I see nothing new."

"Thanks, Tuck." Jerry pointed to the printer. "That little printer seems to be working great. This printout is good quality."

"It should be. YOU paid enough for it," Tuck answered, smiling.

Buddy had heard the conversation and started laughing. "Tuck says he ain't cheap, but he is!" he quipped, they all joined in the laughter. The one thing you could count on from this crew was professional work, and lots of joking to keep the spirits up. Everyone here knew that possibly a human life was hanging in the balance and they all desperately wanted some answers.

The whole crew was now looking to Jerry to find out the latest locally. Of course, all eyes switched to the door when a man in uniform stepped through and scanned the crowd, and then obviously centered on their tables. He walked straight over to the crew, without hesitation. "I deduct this is the crew working with one Jerry Wiley. I *know* that because I know all those old folk over there," he indicated the seniors, "and y'all are new to Lenoir. Strangers, one might conclude." He smiled. "I am Billy Rankin, Deputy Sheriff, and the one chosen to come see what I can learn here. The sheriff gets upset when a felony happens in his territory. I am supposed to represent him until he can get with y'all."

Jerry stepped forward, offering his hand, which Billy took. "Deputy, I am Jerry Wiley. Thank you for coming by. I am bragging, and this is a fact: these guys are some of the best investigative minds in the USA, maybe the world; they have solved hundreds of complicated cases." With that, Jerry introduced the whole group. "I know you are familiar with voice analysis. Here is a copy of our man's report. I suggest you take a seat over there and call the number listed with the report. That is the number of Mary Ann Kirkman, the lady we suspect has been taken against her will. You should listen to the message she recorded on her answering machine. After that, form your own analysis, and then read the report. We will talk afterward."

After Billy was seated, J. Leon motioned Jerry over. "Buck and I were looking at the resulting planes that came up with the search using one of Josh's programs. I entered the numbers with wild cards as the last two positions. We got thirty-five hits."

"So what do you have after culling the obvious?"

"What did I tell you, Buck? This guy won't give you time to gloat. Okay Jerry, we have seven possibles, but our best guess is this Beechcraft Duke out of Sarasota, Florida."

"The tail Number is N-198JR. It appears to be a rental. The computer is about to give us the name and phone number of the owner."

"Sounds good. I am sure your reasoning is logical and probably correct. This is good."

"We are not culling the others, as you say, just using a little logic. The others are privately owned planes. Not likely they would use their own plane for mischief. Of course, folks have been known to 'modify' their numbers if mischief is planned. We will follow through with some internet checks and phone calls and if necessary, we will do a go-see ourselves. I might take Buck along just for muscle."

Buck began to change color; he was easily embarrassed.

"Can you get pictures of the seven?"

"We have them, no problem," responded J. Leon.

"Let's get Melvin Peace back to look at the pictures."

"Good idea, I am sure a local law dog can round him up."

"I'll talk to Billy; meanwhile, we have a spot for a Command Center at the local motel. We need to move there. Maybe Billy can be locating Melvin, and get him over to the motel."

Jerry told everyone to pause their individual activities so they could relocate to the motel. He explained the set up. A couple of the guys ordered something to take back to the motel. About that time, Billy came over to Jerry and handed him the report. "It has been a while since I have seen the speech analysis, but listening to the lady on the phone, I would have to agree completely with the report."

He handed the analysis back to Billy. "Here, keep it. You can start your file on the case. The phone analysis is a good start. I am sure the FBI will want a copy as well. Our crew has located what they think is the plane used last night. We would like to run all the pictures by old Melvin to see if he agrees. Billy, what I really want you to see is the professionalism in this group. So I want you to observe the first 'lineup presentation' with a witness. I think you will learn to appreciate this crazy bunch in a while."

"Do you want me to find Melvin? I know the old guy and usually where he hangs out?"

"That would be great; we will be in the motel suite, number nine. I will leave word for the FBI agents if they come here. They might just call first, who knows?"

Billy smiled with agreement concerning the 'who knows' statement, threw a quick friendly salute to Jerry, and headed for his cruiser. The rest of the crew was wrapping up and heading out to the parking lot.

As this was happening, Sherry had found a quiet spot and spent some time quietly praying for Mary Ann to have strength. She prayed for her safety and, most of all, for her return. Sherry wanted terribly to hug that girl right now. Her mind went back to the time when she'd been kidnapped, becoming the victim, a very dark time of her life in the small country of Belize. It had been a terrible time; one in which she had been dragged around like a rag doll. A time that she was unable to match the strength of a mad man, "Oh God, *PLEASE* give her strength!" she said aloud.

"Honey... honey, we are leaving now."

Coming back to the present, she nodded at her husband.

With extension cords, lamps, extra chairs, and folding tables furnished by motel management, a Command Center was quickly set up. Now, from the van, they had more sophisticated computer gear, printers, and plotters. Satellite tracing was set up with video feed. Work began again in earnest.

While the crew was relocating and setting up, Sherry and Buck made a run to the local grocery store for several juices, fruit, coffee, sandwich stuff, and a myriad of things. She had learned over the past couple years with them, what kept these guys fueled. Buck was familiar with a local bakery stocked up on sticky-buns, the real fuel of the MVA.

She and Buck returned at about the same time Sheriff's Deputy Billy Rankin was pulling into the motel parking lot. Billy had found Melvin. When they saw Sherry and Buck needed help, they assisted and the car was emptied in no time. As Rankin stepped into the room with a load in his arms, he nearly dropped the lot. He had not seen this much electronics since his short FBI training. Jerry walked over and relieved him of some of the supplies.

"My wife knows what this crew needs, Billy, and she wants them running in high gear. This should do it."

"Great command and control room you guys have here. You sure do move fast," he said, obviously impressed. "I nearly forgot; you did want Melvin here, right?"

"Absolutely. I think Leon needs to talk to Melvin. Let's stand back and watch."

J. Leon had already been talking to Melvin; he was briefed on the procedure. They were sitting at a large video display. J. Leon positioned Melvin directly in front of the screen. "Now Mel, as I said, I want you to look at ten or fifteen air planes. Do not answer at first; I just want to flash each one in front of you for about 3 seconds. After the first run, I will repeat them again about the same speed. All I want is a NO if you are positive that I have a plane that is NOT the one you saw. Remember, if you are not sure say nothing, got it?"

"Yep, fire away."

As the pictures went past, Melvin's body language told Leon that Melvin had seen three that jarred a memory. "Now Mel, let's go through them again. Remember, we are only culling now. Here they come."

"No." Pause. "No … No." This went on until Melvin had culled all but three planes.

"Very good, Melvin. Would you like a soda or some juice or coffee?" Leon asked.

"I did see some grapefruit juice, when we brung in the groceries, 'at made my mouth water."

Everyone was watching the show, so Buddy volunteered and quickly brought over a glass of grapefruit juice in ice. Melvin grinned. "You wouldn't happen to have some salt and a dash of vodky, would you?"

"I can sure get some salt, but I think that dog is out today," Buddy replied, referring to the Salty dog Mel was craving.

"Then I guess that will have to do." Mel laughed. He added salt and took a big swallow. He was clearly enjoying being the center of attraction.

"Ready Mel, I am going to run the three we have left by you. Tell me what you think about them. I will leave it up as long as we need it. Check this one out first, it is a 1979 Cessna 340A. What do you think?"

"That does look like it, but I think there are too many winders on the side."

"Okay, the next one is a 2001 Seneca V. How does that look?"

"Too much black I think, but it went by pretty fast."

"Okay, take your time. We can always go back and take another look."

"Here we have a Beechcraft Duke. What do you think?"

"I think 'at's it but now I am not as sure."

"No problem. I want you to look back at the screen. What do you see?"

"Hey man, how did you do that? At's the airport across the street from ma house." Melvin was not the only one impressed; everyone was smiling.

"Now what I want to do is take a minute and get some perspective. I am going to raise you up. Well, not actually raise you up but lower the runway. When it gets about like you see it from your place, let me know."

"Hey, this is somethin'. Take 'er down a little more. I can see their 'chemley', clear. There, you got it."

A loud knock sounded on the door. Tuck walked over to answer. "May I help you?"

"Probably, we need to see Doctor Jerry Wiley. We understand he is here."

"He is, but he is very busy."

"Is he too busy for the FBI?" came the sarcastic question.

"I'll tell you what, FBI. If you can keep the noise down, you can step inside. We are about to find out some very important information. You might even be interested. Shucks, you might learn something, but with your attitude, I doubt it. Maybe you ought to wait outside." At that point, the other agent stepped forward—a female agent.

"I am Agent Angela Mix. We were told there was a suspected kidnapping here in Caldwell County and Dr. Wiley had information about it. We are talking a federal offense, so we need to talk to him NOW."

Knowing it was probably the FBI, Jerry had walked to the door. "Please do not take this wrong, but we are at a crucial point in our investigation. If you would like to respectfully join us, you are welcome. What will it be?"

"Doctor, I am not used to taking orders from civilians, no matter their title. Was there a kidnapping and what proof do you have? The FBI does not play games. Being educated, you do know the word obstruction, do you not?"

"Excuse me a minute," he said, turning to the group inside. "Hold everything and let Mel finish his grapefruit juice. The rest of you take a break." Jerry took out his cell phone and dialed. The other party answered the call in short seconds. "This is Doctor Wiley. I need to speak with Agent in Charge Beatty." Listening, the first agent started to say something, but Jerry froze him with a look and spoke into the phone. "No ma'am, that will not do.

This is an emergency concerning a couple of his agents who seem to carry a chip on their shoulder. Please tell him I enjoyed our conversation, and I mean no disrespect, but I am calling Assistant Director Burns. I will get back to him later. Thank you for your time." Jerry stepped outside, past the agents.

He hung up and dialed the assistant director's private number. Agent Mix held up a stop signal. Jerry shook his head as he heard a familiar voice on the other end. "Okay, what is the square root of eighteen hundred fifty six?" Burns answered. "You finally got that right. Of course it's me. How many people have your private number?..... Are you enjoying your new job? ... Yeah I feel for you, and yes I want a favor. Why else would I call?" Jerry smiled, while Agent Mix waved a give up signal, a gesture soon mirrored by the other agent.

"Honestly Tom, Assistant Director Tommy Burns has a good ring to it and I am so very proud of you. Now to business, I am sure a very good friend has been kidnapped. I contacted Beatty and he said no problem, he would send two of his best. Now what I want to know is, would he lie to me and send me two incompetent crapheads?" ....

As Burns spoke, he looked purposefully at the agents, who stood there, their faces flushed. "I'll take your word for it because I don't know Beatty, but if there is a problem I will bother you again. And Tommy, thanks friend, your math is getting better give my love to that pretty wife."

Before either agent could speak, Jerry ended the call and said, "I am glad you stopped by. I am sure you were told that this is only a heads up. We all know that no real kidnapping happens unless the person is missing three days. We also know a trail gets cold in three days. That is why my crew and I are here. Now, if you want to listen and share information you are welcome inside with no hard feelings; otherwise, you can leave and when it is declared a 'real' kidnapping, we will turn over all our information to you. This is not a territorial squabble. It is a human life we are talking about. This crew will not be bothered by something silly like 'LOOK AT ME, I'M SOMEBODY'. What you heard was not a power play; it was to let you know I am very serious. Is that understood?"

"Yes sir, but…"

"No buts, let's start all over. I am Doctor Jerry

Wiley." He held out his hand. "And you are?"

"Agent Mix here, Doctor. Glad to meet you, I think."

"Agent Taft, sir. I hope we can be of service."

"I think we can work together. Now inside we have a man who saw a plane take off. We feel very sure Mary Ann Kirkman was on that plane. Mary Ann is the one missing. One of our men is finishing up the plane ID lineup. Come on in."

Inside all eyes went to the door. "Crew, these are Agents Mix and Taft. Since this case is not official, they have volunteered to see how much merit the case has so far. Sorry for the interruption. Leon, let's continue… Okay."

"Now Mel, this is very important. What first got your attention yesterday evening?"

"It wuz 'at big pickup truck startin' to turn around, but instead of turning around he drove right down the runway. That sucker turned around and left his flashers on like he was gonna take off like an airoplane."

"Was it something like this?" a dark form

appeared on the screen and went to the end of the runway showing a blinking light. Leon put a pair of glasses on Mel, then handed a few around—all made of cheap pasteboard and celluloid. "Now this is important: I am going to make that truck fly like it was plane. I want you to tell me if it should it be higher or lower. Watch."

The black spot came forward, and Mel yelled and ducked. "How the heck did you do that?"

"Not important. Do I need to raise the plane higher?"

"Yeah, I think so."

"Okay, what I am going to do is repeat the take off, over and over again until it looks like the takeoff you have seen; so just sit there, don't duck and tell me when you think it looks right. Here goes."

After a couple of minutes, Mel pointed at the screen. "Dat's it!" he said, astonished, and even more so when Leon changed the color of the truck to white and adjusted the lighting to what it was that night.

"Now Mel, I did all that to prepare for this final

test. Sit there and think about last night. Now I am going to fly those planes by you. Don't say anything, just watch them."

After he got the planes to fly on screen, Leon asked, "Do you want to do it again?"

"Sure, but I know a'ready which one it wus … it wus number two. I know I said number three, but I wus wrong, it wus number two. But fly 'em agin. I like this."

After the final run, they all took the glasses off and Mel again apologized for mixing the planes up.

Leon smiled at Melvin. "I'll let you in on a secret. You did not mix them up. I intentionally shuffled the planes to get a better gauge of your memory. You did great, Mel, and thanks for coming back down. You have been a great help." Everyone thanked him, shook his hand and patted him on the back with big smiles on their faces. Melvin loved all the attention, especially upon feeling another bill being deposited in his hand by Jerry with a loaded handshake.

"Wait Melvin, and I will give you a ride back home," the deputy sherriff called out.

"Ats all rite, Sheriff. I need to walk and it ain't but a few miles. 'Sides, I'm thinking about shopping fer a new hat." Melvin shut the door, looked at the bill, and found it to be another hundred. He jumped up in the air, clicked his heels together, and yelled, "YeeHA!"

CHAPTER 7

WE HAVE FOUND THE PLANE

After Mel departed, Jerry got Mix and Taft, along with Rankin, and introduced them to each other as law enforcement. "I want you guys to know I appreciate any input you can give my men until it becomes your investigation. As of right now, with only what we know for sure, I am positive Mary Ann is in deep trouble. I would cooperate with the terrorists, if required to get her back. We will uncover much of the same things you guys would have found, if you were allowed to start a full investigation with the backing of your individual units. With that said, you will get EVERYTHING we uncover and learn. My daddy once said, 'a person can accomplish a lot, if he doesn't care who gets the credit'. Daddy was right; I have learned that the hard way. So I am speaking as a friend of Mary Ann's: I don't care who finds her and brings her home to her family, breathing and in one piece—I just want her found. This is off the record, as they say. I want it to go no further, but if a ransom will get her back, I will pay it, then I will blow the culprits to Hell along with the money. Now can we be on the same page here?" Heads nodded in agreement.

"You might know what we have here, but if not, let me go over it. We have satellite monitoring and live video. I have men who can get into any database and back out without leaving a trace. By the way, it is only done in the interest of justice. I have linguists and martial arts experts. We have access to, or we can buy the latest in technology.

"We are checking right now on the suspected plane. None of us expect much from that because it is probably a rental under false ID and names. We are now checking for businesses in the area with monitoring systems along US-321 in hopes we can get the tag number of the Hummer. We pray they went through a drive thru and we can catch the video before the video recycle starts. I have called in some more people to do the leg work."

"Doctor, just to be clear," Mix cut in, "the FBI will not reimburse your expenses, and I am sure the local law enforcement units will not, just to make sure that is up front."

"I do appreciate your concern, but these men and women would work at their own expense. This is a friend of my wife that is missing, and she means a lot to her. I keep using the term 'my crew'; in actuality, they are no longer obligated to me. They did work for and with me for many years, but my company has been disbanded, dissolved for a few years now. We are friends. They know I will cover all expenses, but I also know they would even pay to help. We were unique, the best."

"Why have I never heard of you and your crew?" Taft asked.

"First of all, I am sure every contact on record with my organization, 'The MVA', is sealed. I was once a CIA agent myself. I doubt if you would even be allowed to read the files. I'm not being elusive, just factual. You did not hear of us publicly, and that just might be because we all followed my daddy's advice: make it right, provide justice, and forget the applause; it is the deed that counts. You did not hear because we lived that principle. We got results and the good deeds were our pay and applause. Stick around and you may learn that."

"Excuse me Boss," Leon said. "We are checking on the plane now, if you want to monitor. I am using the satellite phone and the speakers so everyone can hear." They all could hear the phone ringing.

"Thompson Transportation, Thompson here, can I help you?"

"Mr. Thompson, this is Leon 'Jacoby'." He winked at Buddy, who smiled at his choice of names. "I was looking at the register. Do you still have the Beechcraft Duke, and do you lease or rent the plane?"

"Well, Mr. Jacoby, you ask a hard question there. I still own the aircraft, she is a sweet thing too; however, it is overdue back on a rental."

"Shucks, I am up in North Carolina and thinking of flying down. I wanted to borrow the Duke for a couple days just to try it out."

"I sure wish it was back. I am getting a little antsy because insurance in Florida is high enough without adding a damage claim. I am sitting here hoping it isn't sitting somewhere needing help."

"How long did the guy rent it for and who was it? And could you call me when he brings it back, if it is flyable of course." Leon added the last with a little humor in his voice.

"I can't give out the name information, Mr. Jacoby, privacy you know, but it was rented five days ago for five days. The guys shoulda been in yesterday evening or early this morning. I will probably get a call and explanation; that is not common, but it ain't unusual in this business. I will certainly call you. Give me that number."

"Just to make sure I am looking at the right plane, is the tail number N dash one ninety-eight JR? And are you still in Sarasota?"

"Yep, that is her number all right, and we are not actually in Sarasota. We are at the Sarasota-Bradenton International Airport. It's the old Army Air Force landing field that has been extensively modified. SBIA even has a Port Of Entry Authorization. We are on the small hangar side; shingle outside says Thompson Transportation. I sure hope we can do business, Mr. Jacoby."

"Yeah, me too." Leon gave him the phone number. "Please give me a call just as soon as you hear something on the Duke."

"Willco on that, have a good day up in Carolina." And the call ended.

"Okay, what are your impressions?"

The group brainstormed a little, most agreeing the plane was now gone, and Mr. Thompson would never see it again. "It would be too much to hope for that Thompson has a video set up in his office, wouldn't it?" Others were thinking the same.

Stella was sitting over by the window listening to the group.

"Stella," Jerry said. "Are you ready for a flight to Florida?"

"I knew you'd say that. I already sent a text to Vickie to get the bird ready. I am waiting on her answer now, but yes of course I am born to be in the air, you know that. I am headed next door to prepare a flight plan." The law enforcement guys were a little caught aback at the beautiful brown-eyed girl being the pilot who had landed Dr. Wiley's jet on the local runway.

"Buddy, it is you or Tuck. Leon 'Mr. Jacoby' wanted to go but needs to be checking his satellites. Get the description of the guy who rented it of course and if there is possibly a video anywhere, get it, buy it, borrow it; you know better than me what we need. Stella said roughly two hours flying time. Take what you need. Whenever you get back, I hope we have more of this mystery put together."

"Buddy will do it. The sucker could talk the Devil out of a match. Sticky is even slicker, but he ain't here." Tucker laughed.

"Sherry just took a call from Matt. He and Luke will be here in fifteen minutes. They just cleared Hickory. Josh and Megan will be here in an hour or so. She took a couple vacation days to be with him since they are newlyweds." He was interrupted with cat calls, ah's and oh's. "We need that list of businesses that have surveillance cameras so they can start their search."

J. Leon had already fired up the computer and associated it with the satellites. The large screen lit up, showing some live tracks of air craft. Each blip had a number, airline, and destination blinking as well. One or two blinked MIL for military. The FBI agents fastened their gazes on the screen while Rankin walked over to Jerry. "Doctor, would it be possible for me to accompany Buddy to Florida?"

"Billy, call me Jerry. What do you think the sheriff would say, and how soon can you get out of that uniform? But to answer your question, it is okay with me. I am sure Buddy would not mind, but only with the sheriff's blessings."

Billy's slipped out his cell phone as Jerry finished speaking, and speed dialed the sheriff. After a short time, his lips curved in a smile. "Thanks, Sheriff, these guys know what the heck they are doing."

"Jerry, I have some sports clothes in the cruiser if I can use the bathroom to change."

"Do it. Buddy and Stella will be waiting. Can you drive and leave the cruiser at the airport?"

"Absolutely." Rankin nodded, still smiling, as he

headed for his change of clothes.

"Hey, boss," Leon called from the satellite station. Jerry walked over. "My guys had left one of our 'eyes'—that is what they call the satellites—over the area of Georgia West. The memory can record up to thirty days. This is last night; time clock is on the screen, Eastern Standard Time. So about seven last night. Look at this." About fifty miles west of Atlanta, a blip was showing 'UFO'. J. Leon said one of his guys programmed in UFO on any plane with no known flight plan. "Now keep in mind this is not unusual during daylight hours, with planes flying less than two hundred miles an hour, because they will be small plane owners up for a day or crop dusters and they are usually flying low. You are seeing a UFO at eighteen thousand feet, flying 350 mph. His heading will take him a little east of Sarasota, but since we know he did not land, or at least we know he did not return the plane, if this is our guy, he was still most likely going to Florida."

"How much of a description can you get of the plane?" Mix asked.

"Well, I can be general and make an educated guess. It isn't a 747. My techie can do a little better but he cannot say it is THE plane. Now when Josh gets here, he might be able to ease into FAA and we might get more solid information. At least I hope so."

"This is amazing that amateurs can have this much technology," Taft said, which elicited Mix giving him 'the look'.

"Taft, I won't explain this again. These men are more experienced than you or your immediate superior, Agent in Charge Beatty. They have been through FBI training, Seal and CIA training. Leon here OWNS the satellites he is using. He has put his life on the line more times than I like to count. Now I want you and Agent Mix to go outside and talk. I would suggest you listen to her. My friend's life is on the line and I will call the president if I have to and have you removed. I want cooperation, and I will give the same, but I will not allow you to belittle one of the best in the business. I am not petty enough to threaten; please remember that. I am one easygoing guy." Jerry turned and walked over to where Tucker was compiling the list of surveillance cameras in the area as Mix lead Taft outside.

Outside, she just stared at Taft for a few seconds. "Tommy, do you think these guys know what they are doing?"

"Sure, what is eating the doc? I am amazed at what they can accomplish."

"You are smarter than this. To use the word 'amateur' is a slap in the face. Do you think they went to Radio Shack and bought all this stuff? You are seeing cutting edge technology. If you are smart, you won't say too much. I do not want to be pulled off this job. This is going to be a good ride and I can bet you, we can learn something."

"Sorry Mix, I reckon I am having a Joe Biden day."

"Also, Beatty did not tell us much about the doctor. Did you know he is a billionaire and that is with a 'B', Tommy? To me that means he is serious, he is working, and not sitting at the country club calling these guys to see how it is going as he sips a cocktail. The victim here is Mary Ann Kirkman, your run of the mill middle class lady. I like it when the top one percent takes interest in the forty-five percent, don't you? Now let's get back inside before we miss something."

CHAPTER 8

WHERE AM I?

The plane landed and rolled to a stop. Although still sitting blindfolded, Mary Ann sensed someone beside her. Nothing had been said to indicate where she was, nor why.

I guess this is what you call a kidnapping ... but why me? Frightened beyond words, she reached near panic stage. Very few words had been spoken, even when she was given the note to record on her answering machine. She had stood in shock when the strange man hit all the right buttons and turned the correct knobs to begin the recording, while she could not change her own message without re-reading the instructions.

Mary Ann's life had not been a bed of roses. Over her seventy years, she experienced many set-backs in her life, relationships, and health. But, despite all of that, she was blessed with a wonderful family—the one thing she had desperately wanted from childhood, and the reason she had quit school to marry and have children. She had given birth to Debbie, Robyn and her main man, Dusty. Having the girls was amazing enough, and then Dusty's appearance just rounded out the sweet brood. Raising them had been her dreams come true she regretted nothing, not even the bad times. Hers were good kids. She let her mind drift to the memories of her most precious moments with them...

Of course they were good kids. I was their mama, wasn't I?

Then the tears started to fall. Again.

Being a woman of faith, with prayer and Bible reading always a big part of her life, she set about praying her heart out. How else could she deal with this strange turn of events?

The kids are grown and have their own families. But I have always been there... What will they do now? What will they think? Will they assume I just found some man and ran off? Oh Lord, now there is my sweet Buck, will you wonder about me? You really don't know how I feel about you, my hunk. Hey, what the heck. I don't know if I am going to live or die, so I guess I'll just go ahead and admit it—I bet you would be sweet in bed.

She cried and cried some more. It seemed an eternity since she had been dragged from her safe haven on top of the mountain.

When this all started, she had been thinking of Buck, that he had probably finished his golf game. She'd smiled at the fleeting thought of taking up golf so she could start going with him. Then, the knock came at her door, one that would forever shatter her feelings of safety. A knock on one's door proved such a rare occurrence up on the peak, it being a safe, gated community—not even Jehovah's Witnesses would show up. There had never been a problem in Greening Heights, so she opened the door without hesitation. That moment of carelessness had turned her heaven into a hell. The shock overcame her, so sudden, she could not think or react. She was violently pushed back into the room so she lost her footing and fell backwards; then, she heard the door being slammed shut. She found herself looking up into the barrel of the largest handgun she had ever seen. Being a Southern girl, she was familiar with fire arms, and even more so since Dusty had become a LEO. From behind the gun, a man spoke, his words accented. She recognized that accent as Hispanic.

"I do not want to hurt you lady, but I will not hesitate to do so if you do not follow my every instruction. Do you understand?"

Her first impression was to answer in Spanish in an attempt to gain his sympathy and trust, as was her nature, but she immediately dropped the idea, answering him with a nod of her head.

"I understand what you said, but—"

Her phone rang. He held up his hand, bringing the gun an inch or two closer.

"You will answer and say that you do not feel well and cannot talk, is that clear?"

Mary Ann nodded. He picked up the phone and hit speaker, then handed it to her.

"Hello."

"Hi Mary Ann, I just wanted to chat. Is this a bad time?"

"No sweetie, but I am just feeling a little down. Guess I am just missing Calbie. You know how sweet and understanding he always was. I was getting ready to wash my hair, so I better go. Bye…"

"Bye, Mary Ann, I love you." Sherry said to a dial tone.

"You understood what I said. At present that is all that is needed," the intruder said when she hung up. "We will first tell everyone why you no longer answer your phone. You will place this message on your answering machine. Do you understand? Just nod your head." She did. Once the man had set the answering machine to record, she read the note he handed her. It was obvious to her at that point, they were going outside and for some reason, she grabbed Dusty's photo off the mantel. The little guy slapped her and motioned her to put it back. Thinking quickly, she placed it at the end of the row. For the first time, her kids' pictures were not positioned in order of birth. It wasn't much of a clue, but it was something.

As they left, the man—small in stature but was big in intimidation skills—used her keys to lock the door before leading her down the steps to the sidewalk, where he pushed her into the back seat of a big black pickup. A big man was waiting inside, sitting in the driver's seat. Without saying a word, he started the truck and soon they were off, with the driver carefully observing the slow speed limit of Greening Heights. No one paid any attention as the gate opened automatically for the departing 'guests'; Just another family going out for a sandwich or ice cream.

No one in the truck spoke during the trip. Both men kept smoking; the driver lowered the windows to clear the smoke.

I guess it is a rental and they don't want to pay extra for the smoke smell. Mary Ann did not mind smoke. She had kicked the habit herself but still enjoyed the smell of a cigar, cigarette or pipe. All of a sudden, she thought of her cell phone… *Can I call 911?* The guys did not seem to be paying her any attention; maybe she could get away with it. Carefully, she eased it out of her pocket, but when she turned it on, the thing beeped. The little guy turned, with fire in his eyes he grabbed for the phone. He was not quite fast enough as Mary Ann just threw it out the window.

Leaning over, he slapped her and laughed. "Someone will find it this week and sell it for a dollar, stupid bitch."

When they left Zack's Ford Road, the turns indicated they were going toward Blowing Rock, but then the truck had turned into the little airport. The rest was a blur, the plane coming directly toward them on the runway. When she was forced out and into the plane, she knew this meant BIG trouble. Inside the plane, she was buckled in and blindfolded. Flying was not her favorite thing, but as the plane took off, she realized it was the least of her worries.

After a long time, her stomach told her they were landing; it was like going over a whoop de doo on the road. They were now on the ground and she was just sitting there. Her hands were not bound and she started to move the blindfold but someone stopped her—the little guy again. "No, no pretty lady, leave it in place until someone removes it for you. Just sit there, it will not be long now."

More voices could be heard outside the plane, the door was opened, and she heard the words, "Remove her blindfold, I want to see what you have brought me, my friend."

The blindfold was taken off and her eyes

adjusted to the semi-darkness; dawn was just breaking.

She stared in the face of a dark-complexioned man standing outside the plane offering his hand to her. Once on the ground, she looked around. "Where am I, and why am I here?"

"Ah, Mrs. Kirkman, you are just as beautiful as in your pictures. I will answer all your questions, but first let's go inside. I know you are very familiar with golf carts, so let's ride up to the hacienda."

The little man spoke to the new man, "Amigo, what about the plane?"

"Put it in the barn. It will get a new paint job and papers. I like this one." He turned back to Mary Ann.

Golf carts had certainly been a big part of her life. That was the main mode of transportation at Greening Heights; *Will I ever see my golf cart and home again?* During the ride, she surveyed the place. They were in a mostly flat area, and it was much warmer than the North Carolina Mountains. The fields were green and spotted with cattle. She recognized palm trees in the fields and along the road. The home looked like the plantation homes in old pictures and some in Charleston, SC. Four tall white columns and a lot of fancy trim work addressed the front. When they arrived, they were met by a man in a porter's uniform. He graciously helped her out of the cart and the man who had brought her there rushed to her side; together, they climbed the steps and entered a beautifully decorated home.

"Please be seated." She sat at a huge dining table, her favorite breakfast laid out in front of her—a croissant, poached egg, and coffee. "I will have coffee and then leave us," the man instructed. The uniformed man seemed to head to the kitchen.

Once they were alone, he spoke. "Now, Mrs. Kirkman, I know this is all very disconcerting to you…"

For the first time, Mary Ann found her tongue. "Not so," she cut in. "This is an average day for me, being shanghaied like a drunken sailor, dragged out of my own home by someone I do not know, and placed on a plane. You probably know I hate to fly. Then I am landed in Ethiopia or some unknown place in someone's cow pasture. No man, this is a normal day in Mary Ann's life." Mary Ann was shaking as she finished.

"Believe me, Mary, I do understand. Now let me introduce myself. I am Andrew. Whether you know it or not, things are good, and I see you still have fire and a sense of humor. I know you are hungry, so try to relax and eat. You will find the coffee to be the best you have ever tasted. Now silence and you listen."

Andrew poured his coffee from the same pot from which Mary Ann's coffee had been served; she took note of that. "Now, I will call you Mary. Mary, I want you to know that if you cooperate, this can be the best thing that ever happened. You will be very happy, I assure you. You will enjoy things beyond your wildest dreams."

"Excuse me, Andrew. I was very happy. Life was finally being good to me. That was until your roughnecks came along. Now what happens if I do not cooperate?"

He shook his head. "Then, my dear, it will be very unpleasant for a while, but in the end, you will cooperate and you will enjoy the same life I described. But for some time you may require a few needle marks, if you fail to oblige."

"I cannot see me cooperating and not knowing if I will see my family again. Can I call them?"

"I'm afraid not, but they will be fine. There was no trace of you leaving. It seems as if the earth swallowed you. You are a smart lady. What would have happened if you had died on top of your mountain last night? Think of it. Your children would cry. They would have to go through the procedures of funeral and burial. They would know you were gone, dead and buried."

"Isn't that normal? They would have closure."

"Strange, that new concept of 'closure', but it is just a word, Mary; you would still be gone. What I am offering, to you and them, is release. I am going to give you a new life, a new name and riches. You will never want for a thing for the remainder of your life. And as to your children, they will not see you in the ground, but in their minds you will be somewhere alive. They will anticipate seeing you come home. They will have hope, something they would not have if you were buried."

"You are telling me that I am going to live here in this house as your wife, concubine, whore—whatever—and never see my kids again?"

"Oh, the American mind, sex and so on. No, my dear Mary, this is just to be a training school. Unless you force me, you will never be molested. During the next month to six weeks, you will become Mrs. Mary LaRoach. You will have a new life, complete with Social Security Number, birth certificate, driver's license, and past history; very simple really. I want you to cooperate without becoming a zombie. Mary, please believe me, I can create a zombie, but it is not in either of our best interests. I want you as your real vibrant self. You will have servants, but you will still crochet and sew, because Mary LaRoach does those things. You can even cook if you have a mind to. You will live in a mansion, not a country home like this. Your home will have a pool, spa, and your own trainer and hair stylist. Does this sound interesting at all, Mary?"

"Mister, that sounds like a nightmare. I have always been Mary Ann. I lived as Mary Ann, and I will die as Mary Ann. So you may as well kill me now, because I am not becoming Mary LaRoach for you or anyone else," she said, shaking harder now. Immediately, she pushed back from the table, jumped up faster than she realized she could, and ran back towards the front door.

Out of nowhere appeared two strong, muscular young women, both dark-skinned and very quick. They caught her firmly by both arms, one lady on each side. Trying with all her might, she could not budge. Finally, she gave up, and they escorted her back to the table. Andrew clapped his hands lightly. "Bravo, Bravo, Mary LaRoach. I expected no less." Offered the same chair she'd been seated in, she sank down in it. "However, Mary, this will be your first lesson. I hope it is the last." He nodded to the ladies. Out came a black circle of plastic with two metal prongs. Mary Ann could not see the women, but she knew they were moving to her side. When the prongs touched her back, she screamed when she felt what seemed like fifty thousand volts of energy coursing through her; she had never before felt that much pain in an instant. *Surely they have killed me...* The women held her steady so she stayed in the chair. She couldn't move even if she wanted to. For a long couple of minutes, she dealt with the agony, until her old self, Mary Ann, came back to the present. She had just been Tasered. Her mind went back to the day Dusty had accepted a Taser to carry. The rules were: any LEO that carries a Taser must first be hit by one; the point being, having felt it, you will know exactly what will happen when you use it on someone. Dusty had said he never again wanted to be hit by one, and in her mind she said, *Amen, Dusty.*

"That, Mary LaRoach, is the *easy lesson*; you will find that I do not exaggerate. Missie and Mae will be with you as companions for a while. They will take you to your room. You probably need to relax in a bubble bath for an hour or so and do some serious thinking. The girls will draw your bath and give you a massage beforehand. I want there to be no misunderstanding, so you should know that every part of this house is covered with cameras. Because you are a lady, only other women will observe you during your private times, but you must know I am protecting an investment so I am very concerned that you do yourself no harm. I will only observe when you are fully dressed or I am called by one of the ladies because of an emergency. We will talk again later, maybe at the evening meal."

Nothing else was said. The girls helped her out of the chair and guided her upstairs to a large spacious room. One of the girls helped her get undressed down to her panties and bra, and then directed her to the massage table. With scented exotic oils, she was given the first professional massage she had ever experienced. In spite of her position, it felt good. Some of her favorite music was playing over the speakers, but so far the girls had not spoken. The bubble bath came next in a bubbling spa; the water was hot and felt great against her aching body.

Mary Ann lay thinking, knowing she was on camera, and knowing no one could invade her mind. *I have got to figure this out. What in the world is happening back home? Has anyone missed me yet? I hope the kids notice the out of order pictures; it will be confusing but it is something. BUT what can they do, report me missing? I think I saw someone on Zack's Ford Road as I threw the phone. My only hope is someone finds it that is honest, and not interested in that buck. But I guess it shattered in a thousand pieces anyway. Oh Buck, just when I thought I had found the jewel of my life, someone I don't even know wants to change it all...*

With the constant moving of the water and the relaxing bubbles, in spite of herself, she drifted off into a fitful sleep.

CHAPTER 9

A QUICK TRIP TO SARASOTA

"You guys are part of an incredible outfit. I want to thank you for a chance to help or at least observe," Rankin said, while they were on the way to the small airport.

"Imma tell you something, Deputy Billy. I hope you have an extra set of skivvies,   'cause Stella here flies like an Alaskan Bush Pilot. The boss has a lot of trouble with her drinking," Buddy said in mock seriousness.

"I'll have you know, Buddy. I had the whole two week crash-course on flying, and I didn't miss but two days. Shucks, I know most of the important knobs are on the dash of that thing. I even know what some of them do and I have a book that tells about everyone of them if I need it. I can start it up, well, with Vickie's help, and I haven't had a drink in an hour, so I'm good."

"*Crash* being the operative word in that sentence

Billy, I'm good with English."

Billy was enjoying this; he could tell this was going to be one great crew to work with.

"About the *incredible outfit*, yeah, we *were* incredible, Billy. Most of the principals involved in the now defunct MVA Corporation have their own investigative services. I have a great company myself, but to tell you the truth I miss the camaraderie and excitement that Jerry can generate. The MVA was very unique. I don't think there ever has been any better."

"Sounds like the MVA is missed. What exactly does that stand for? I am assuming it was some type of investigative service."

"Billy, the MVA meaning of the initials was never published in its non-profit statement. What is stated is that it existed to serve humanity. You know, like stopping a bully on the school yard, that type of thing."

"You aren't gonna tell me, huh?" Billy said, laughing.

Buddy smiled and turned to Stella in the back seat. "The guy *IS* an investigator, ain't he?" They all burst out laughing, just as Billy pulled into the airport. "It is very complicated, Billy. I have a feeling we will probably talk later." Buddy gave him a sly wink.

Vickie directed them where to park as they rolled up. Russell stood on the stoop. Stepping down, he walked over to Stella. "In all seriousness, Stella, you might consider another runway. I do appreciate the business and it looks good from the road to see that plane here, but you might think about a change."

"Russell, I really do understand what you are saying and you can be sure, if I start in and the weather is bad, I will in all probability divert unless there is an emergency. However, Lower Creek is convenient, and it is no big deal with this bird. Most pilots could work it out in good weather. The FAA always errs on the side of logic and safety, and I do agree, in all situations and weather, I would be taking a chance with lives and the boss's ride to force the issue."

"Just stating how I feel. Where are you off to?"

"We are headed to the Sarasota-Bradenton International in Florida. I'm looking for a place to retire." She grinned.

"Your mech said she was riding. Good idea."

"Yeah, for many reasons. Vickie can also fly this bird but she prefers the nuts and bolts."

"Well, you are good to go as far as we are concerned here. Have a good flight."

With everyone aboard, Stella looked at the wind sock and decided to take the same direction the mystery plane had used. Her take off was not going to be for show. But for her own satisfaction, she needed to see just how short she could cut it. The result was just as she thought. "With this baby, I only need half the runway." Below, Russell was giving them the 'thumbs-up'.

Over the intercom, Stella made the standard announcement. "Welcome aboard Wiley Industries World of Flight. We will be heading south at an air speed of five hundred miles per hour. We will be landing at Sarasota-Bradenton International at 1700 hours. Temperature is eighty-three degrees and clear. We are scheduled two and a half hours on the ground. Relax, have a soda; it is a pleasure to serve you."

Looking over at Billy, Buddy took out his phone.

"Time to go to work." He dialed Sarasota. When Mr. Thompson answered, Buddy started his intro. "Ah, Mr. Thompson, Richard here, I am calling for a Mr. Jacoby. I will be in the area later, and he asked me to touch base with you. What time do you usually lock up?"

"I am surprised to hear from Mr. Jacoby. My bird is not back yet, and I explained that to him."

"Oh that? Of course he understood that. He said you were going to call when the Duke was returned, he surely did. But since I work for him and am landing shortly at SBI, he just asked me to look in on you."

"I won't leave here until about six today. With one plane AWOL, I want to give them every chance to avoid extra charges. That is my policy. Stop by, I look forward to it."

"Great, see you in a couple hours, and thanks." Hanging up, Buddy turned to Billy. "Now you asked for this, so you are a part of it. I am going to BS him some, referring to government agencies as the basis. I might ask you to flash a shield, if it becomes necessary. You will be introduced as a deputy sheriff from the beginning. I will not lie, you okay with that?"

"I'm thinking, Buddy, how will it go down?"

"I will small talk him, compliment him on his set-up. Then I am going to tell him the truth and why we are concerned about his plane." Buddy handed Billy his FBI shield. "This is an honorary thing, issued to us by the director himself. There are only twenty-six in existence; five were given to the MVA members."

"I must say that is pretty impressive, along with this plane. It must be sweet, working for a guy who has this."

Buddy got up and went to the cooler. Before opening it, he pressed the intercom button. "Do the drivers need anything to drink? I have Vodka, Wild Turkey, and Jack Daniels, or tomato juice."

"Yeah, Buddy, I want OJ and Vickie wants the tomato juice, thanks."

After delivering to the cockpit, he asked Billy what he wanted. They both were having orange Juice. After a drink of his juice Buddy said, "Here's to success in the land of Orange Juice," and they clicked bottles.

Back in their seats, Buddy explained Jerry's life. Taking his time, he covered Jerry's life's journey— medical school, the position of Head of Medical, the CIA, and his short stint as 'Rags'. At mention of the latter, he covered his and his buddies' relationship to Jerry, and how the four boys had hassled Rags, who turned out to be Dr. Jerry Wiley. "Now, old Tuck back there owes his young life to Jerry. Jerry saved his life by opening him up, reaching in, and massaging his heart. It was like a battlefield or old west operation. Jerry took a sharp pocket knife and a pint of booze from a drunk and operated. Tuck still rubs that scar on his abdomen for luck in tight places."

"If you were kids and knew him in North Carolina and he left and took over Wiley Industries, how did you get back together?"

"That is a sweet story, but one for later. Suffice it to say, he never forgot us. He sorta guided our lives from afar and when we were old enough, he hired us; he also financed all our training. So here I am today, a very satisfied business man in my own right, and willing to do anything for the man I first knew as 'Rags'. The guy I taunted with name calling; I even hit him once with a rock. You will probably meet Sticky, the other member of the club. He owns a big construction company. He was once First Assistant to the NCDOT. You might have heard of him; he was charged with embezzlement by our FBI once. There was nothing to it."

"Are you talking about Mr. Moore, black guy?"

"Yeah, that's Sticky."

"And he was part of the MVA?"

"Oh yeah, a big part, one of the best friends a man could have. Strong dude, prides himself in being able to squeeze a pop can until it burst, knows exactly how many pounds per square inch to apply."

"Well, I be dogged. He hired me once to direct traffic during my off duty time when they were rebuilding US-321, small world."

"Billy about those initials, we have never voiced them around, but I am sure Jerry likes you and I can see approval in his eyes, the letters MVA stand for *Modern Vigilante Association*. Jerry is a straight arrow, he knew an organization like his could turn political or rogue under some leadership, so in the original documents the MVA would be disbanded at his decision or death. He refused to even think of extending it under anyone's leadership other than his. We did not like it as his team, but we knew he was right. I am telling you this in confidence. Not much could be hurt by it, but fact is the name is played close to the vest."

"Buddy, thanks for the vote of confidence and I will honor the terms you laid out. Some day, I would like to hear of some of the operations."

"More than likely you will my friend. I hope this event ends positively." Buddy and Billy sat back both in their own world of thought.

****

"This is your pilot speaking. We will be landing in five minutes. Air traffic is light with no back up. We are a few minutes early. Secure all loose objects and buckle up."

Billy motioned and took Buddy's empty bottle and deposited in a secure trash container, as he was back at his seat buckling in he said, "To tell you the truth, Buddy, this is my first time on any airplane. I think I like flying."

"I like flying myself, but I prefer a classic car."

Billy watched in awe as the landing strip rose to meet them and was surprised that all he heard or felt was the landing gear touchdown. Buddy noticed his surprised look. "Billy, she is good or she would not be working for Jerry."

Over the intercom, Stella said, "Buddy, air control says I can taxi all the way to Thompson's. Want me to do that, or do you want some distance?"

Buddy pressed the seat intercom button. "Take it to his front door, I want him to see the plane and our good looking pilot and co-pilot."

"Roger, but Vickie forgot her bikini!"

About a hundred feet from a temporary berth, Vickie deplaned and closed the plane door. Giving the plane a wide berth, she jogged to the parking spot and guided Stella perfectly into the slot. With the slot's chocks, Vickie chocked the wheels then walked around the wing and gave Stella the thumbs up. Stella cut the engines. Vickie opened the door and pulled out the steps. "Please watch your step. Welcome ashore." Buddy and Billy deplaned, saluted Vickie, and headed for the Thompson business.

Mr. Thompson was just inside the door where he had observed the unfamiliar plane taxi up. "I'm Steve Thompson," he said, holding out his hand.

"Mr. Thompson, I am Richard. Everyone calls me Buddy and this is Deputy Sheriff Billy Rankin of Caldwell County, North Carolina. Nice set up you have here, and I sure like your weather."

"We like it, but evidently you haven't been in Florida in the summer. Few will brag then. The Chamber of Commerce always picks winter to bring folk down to invest." Thompson laughed. "But fellows, you ain't here to talk about the weather. Friend in the tower called when the pilot asked for me. You are flying a Wiley Industries bird and y'all need a Duke like I need a 747. What is it that you really need?"

"You are absolutely right, Mr. Thompson, about us not needing the Duke; however, we do need to locate it and the folks who rented it."

"Something I should know about?"

"Yes sir, there sure is, but first let me thank you for taking me to the point. I truly like that. Now for a good story—back in Caldwell County NC there are two FBI Agents and two other law enforcement groups looking into a kidnapping. Buddy showed his badge to Thompson. It was obvious he only saw *FBI*. Buddy nodded to Billy, who took out his badge. I am here only as a friend, not in any official capacity. Billy is active in the investigation. The missing person is a senior lady, and she was last seen getting into your plane around 1800 yesterday. The Duke's tail numbers N-198JR had landed unauthorized at Lower Creek Airport, a small private airfield. The reason I am here so fast is, the lady is a friend of Mr. Jerry Wiley who owns Wiley Industries, and he told me to take his plane and find out what I can, so here I am."

"When I did not get a call about it being late, I began to get concerned. I probably ain't gonna see that Duke again, am I?"

"In the opinion of six investigators, the ones who leased or rented it will not be returning it. Mr. Wiley said to get any information I could, so we really do need your help. I guess we were dreaming, but I was hoping to see a video camera, but I don't. So, could you fill us in on any description you can jog up about the rental process?"

"Son, you don't see a video camera because I do not want my customers to see a video camera. Some folk are camera shy." Buddy knew he had hit pay dirt because Thompson was grinning. "I have the latest; they are miniatures, posted inside and outside. Would copies suit you?"

"Mr. Thompson, I love it when a man has his bases covered. Copies would be fantastic."

"I can furnish you with copies of the pilot's license and the runt with him. I am sure the names are fakes, but the photos are good."

"Super. I don't want to push, but if you have something they might have touched, and if they signed anything, their handwriting would help."

"Let me tell you something, Buddy. I have a feeling I have lost a plane. I want them caught; I would like personally to kick their butts. So anything we can rustle up, you can have." Turning to the lady over in the far corner bent over the computer with ear phones, he said, "Honey, I am going to need some help over here."

"Just a minute, I am finishing up."

Speaking towards the corner, "Don't shut the

system down," then back to his visitors, "Me and my wife Linda run this place. It is really a Mom and Pop operation. This is my third career. I retired from the flying side of the Marine Corps, then from the nuclear part of the power company. Her daddy couldn't fly a kite, but had a spot here where he rented two little Cessna single engine jobs. We bought him out and he financed it. It was a good deal for all of us." He finished as his wife walked up and he introduced the pair. He told her what he needed and she headed over to the computer.

Both the Thompsons were off, putting together the stuff Buddy had asked for. "Well, this seems to be going well. Is this all we need in Sarasota?" asked Billy.

"Yeah, that about wraps it up for us, and thank goodness sometimes the pieces fall together. *BUT,* if we, that is the whole group, everyone, cannot squeeze out a destination or reason, it is just facts. Albeit anything at this stage is better than nothing, it keeps the momentum going and the juices flowing. Ideas are what we need here." Buddy paused, motioned to a couple chairs and as they sat he asked, "Billy, why are people kidnapped?"

"Ransom, hate, and sex, probably a hundred reasons, but those are the first that jumped in my mind."

"Do any of those make sense in this case?"

"No, her family is not rich, and according to what I have heard and could find on the internet, hate is out, and sex is out in the conventional sense; usually sex kidnappings involve high school or college kids. We have had many examples lately nationwide."

"What I see here is something unique. This was exceedingly well-planned, and it needed money, i.e., the Hummer and the plane, one from hundreds of miles away. The timing was spot on. The Hummer pulls in and almost immediately, the plane lands. Naturally, the plane cannot park and wait; it cannot circle long waiting without drawing attention. Unless in Mary Ann's past, there was some wealthy dude that still carries the hot's for her and has decided to just go get her, there is something else and like Barney Fife would say, 'This is big, Andy, big.' It must be something like an organization or some well heeled gang/group, but for what purpose? That is driving me up the wall!"

Steve Thompson walked back up to the bar-type counter. "Well, gentlemen, this is what we have. The only thing I know that might have a print is the original contract. I carefully made a copy to keep; the original is in this folder. I am not sure, but I might need the original for insurance. Can I get that back?"

"Certainly; just as soon as any definable prints are lifted, we will make a copy, and send this back to you. You will get it back in a plastic shield if the prints were visible. I would leave it there in case the FBI techies want to see it again. I say that because I will not give them your original. As I said, I am not here in an official capacity. Believe me Steve, the FBI will get EVERYTHING you give us. Deputy Sheriff Rankin here will be witness to what we get and he is part of the official investigation. They will get the prints if we find any. You have this on recording, right?"

"You got that right, my man." Steve grinned. "In the folder also are copies of everything I took from them, even a copy of the credit card they gave me."

"Was the credit card good?"

"Of course, you know Linda checked that first

thing."

"Here is a 49GB SanDisk with outside and inside video. The inside will have sound and you can hear they have an accent."

"We won't hold you any longer; I know you want to get home. I hope we not only find these dudes but that your bird is still clean and ready to fly. What do we owe you for this? We have taken your time and supplies."

"Man, you don't owe us anything. Just find these creeps, and if possible, tell me where my bird is."

Buddy smiled in understanding and called across the room to Linda. "Hey Linda, ma'am, could I talk to you a minute?"

Linda walked over.

"It has been a pleasure seeing such a beautiful lady slaving for this guy and not complaining. Mr. Wiley, on the other hand, is an understanding man, and ladies always get his attention, near or far away. He knows time is money, and in this case worth every penny. He sent this down to you." And he handed Linda an envelope.

"You are a silver-tongued sneaky rascal, Buddy, but I like you," Steve said.

Linda gave Buddy a hug. "Give that to Mr. Wiley." She opened the envelope as she walked away. "Whoa, five hundred dollars! We cannot accept this, it is too much."

"There you go, using that 'we' word." Buddy looked around at his partner. "Billy, did I say at anytime, this is for y'all? No sir, I did not. You take that with Mr. Wiley's blessings, but I ain't delivering no hug." They all laughed.

"You don't know what this means to us. We have both been praying. Our youngest daughter is awaiting a kidney. This will help on the insurance co-pay."

"Well, we certainly hope all goes well. Now we have to head back and throw this information out for the team to dissect. You guys have been great, hope to see you soon." They all said their goodbyes and the two men jogged out to the plane.

"Okay, Super Woman, fly us back up north. You have lounged enough in the warmth of Florida, vacation is over," Buddy said as he climbed in the plane. "Ladies, they gave us more than we ever expected. We have video of the crooks. Get us home."

Stella had already been in touch with the tower and had a flight plan with departing time blank. The time was filled in and they were taxiing in eight minutes and in the air in fifteen. At present, life was good. They did wonder about the kidnapped victim though. How was she holding out?

"Billy, it is nice to not have to BS someone to get information." Reaching into his briefcase, he took out his laptop and fired it up. "Let's see what these sleazeballs look like?"

The video was much better than either one expected. The sound was good. "They have the Hispanic accent with their English, but they do not look Mexican. Maybe from South America, even Spain. Matt and Luke can help with that; they are our linguists, among other things. They are the ones who did the voice analysis."

They played it over several times, then all of a sudden, Billy straightened. "Dang it, back in the Thompson's office what did Linda say?" he said.

"She said hug Jerry, the money was too much, but thanks they could use it. They had been praying. What?" Billy stared at Buddy in puzzlement.

"Transplant, organs ... organs are harvested and sold on the black market for thousands."

"I get it, not that this is for the organs. We know no one would go to the expense of this operation for all of the organs from one person. They would go to the next town, or to where the prostitutes hang out, and take one. But yes, this is just another reason for kidnappings, right?"

"You got it. I have no idea what one person sells for, but human trafficking has been going on forever. That is where the word Shanghaied came from—sailors kidnapped for work."

Billy thought for a moment. "Again, it would not be logical to kidnap a senior citizen to sell, would it?"

"Let's mull this over." They sat, letting their minds wander as they cruised back north at five hundred miles an hour. By 2100hrs, they were landing in Lenoir.

CHAPTER 10

CHASING A GHOST PLANE

Since Stella now knew the airport she did not call for any auto lights to help. She used the Lear's landing lights and her expertise to land in the bright moon light. Leaving Vickie to secure the aircraft, Billy drove them back to the motel in the cruiser. As the three walked back into the motel room, as if on cue, yells rang out of:

"How was the vacation?" "Did Stella find Florida?" "I guess we won't have a deputy sheriff around after that trip!" sounded out.

"Okay you jokers, do I ever treat you like this? Imma tell you, when you see what Stella brought back, besides my good looking self, you will show some respect." Smiling, Buddy looked over at Jerry. "We did get some good stuff, probably not enough, but we have pictures and voice prints of the sorry bas—er, rascals." Noticing Matt, Luke, Josh and Megan he said, "Hey guys, good to see you, I hope you have been busy."

"Since you are up, give us a recap, while Leon is

reprogramming for the big screen," were Jerry's instructions.

"We had a good flight, weather was great, and the Thompsons were very cooperative. They do have inside and outside surveillance. After we briefed them on the situation, they gladly made video copies of the renting procedure. Steve, Mr. Thompson, actually gave us the original contract, plus copies of the identification, credit card and license they used to close the contract. I promised him we would return the original contract after Matt and Luke did their magic for prints. He might need it for insurance purposes. He knows that plane is not going to be returned by these guys. Thompson Transportation is a Mom and Pop operation. These are the kind of people you love to deal with; they want justice done also."

"Ready here," J. Leon said.

"Then let's see what we have." Jerry nodded toward Leon.

The video was run three or four times. Most everyone was making notes. There were two flip charts that had been added this evening. "Okay, I know everyone is tired; probably not as tired or worried as Mary Ann is, but we need clear minds if we are going to find her. We need first impressions, then whoever needs sleep can retire, and I do want some of you to do just that. Okay, starting around the room, Leon." They circled the room. Sherry had volunteered to record the comments and combine them for the next day. Following the short brainstorming session, a few hit the sack.

Deputy Sheriff Rankin was still around with Buddy when Jerry joined them. "You guys done well, thanks. Billie the sheriff stopped by, asked me to give you a message—he has no problem with you reporting here for duty until he tells you different. But he does want you to call, and then drop by for a talk."

"Good, that means I am still attached here. Jerry, this is a privilege. I mean that. I want to observe and I hope I can contribute, too."

"Jerry," Buddy spoke up. "I noticed the list over there—'reasons for kidnapping'. We have one more to add, human organs. We do not think in this case it is organs, but maybe something to do with this specific human life. We need a list of unique things in Mary Ann's life. So her friends and family will need to provide that."

"Example, Buddy?" Jerry said as he took a seat.

"Does she speak Swahili? Is she a friend of the president? Does she know any state secrets? Anything, we need to know her complete biography. There is something about Mary Ann that caused someone to spend a lot of money to take her away. I mean these fools picked a seventy year old woman from the Blue Ridge Mountains of North Carolina. There must be something special, or they have taken the wrong person," Buddy answered.

"I think I have something," J. Leon called out. Everyone stopped what they were doing and gathered around the big screen. The display consisted of moving blips; at first glance, this was a satellite display of aircrafts in flight.

"Guys, you are looking at FAA coverage last evening starting at eighteen hundred." Josh brought the Earth's geography into focus. He and Leon worked together. It was Josh's programs that surreptitiously retrieved this info. Josh did not know what a pointing baton was; he used a laser light. Pointing at the screen with his laser, he explained, "This is Lower Creek airport. This, my friends, is Mary Ann inside that blip. Follow her. They swing up into the mountains; they are flying at eight thousand feet. No one pays any attention; notice that there is no ID blip. The ID blip is required by FAA and is called IFF, Identify Friend or Foe. Now watch the magic—the plane glowed red and continued south, they avoid the Atlanta area choosing near Augusta. They then adjust their flight to avoid cities and bases and go over the Okefenokee Swamp in Georgia. Next, they maneuver to avoid Jacksonville, Florida. Then they cross the state and go out over the Gulf of Mexico, but after Tampa, they head inland. They go inland south of Sarasota and we lose them."

"They are lost because they dropped down to less than 1000 feet. Anyone could have seen them, but it is late and that area of Florida is made up of groves, farms and cattle ranches; that is to say, it is sparsely populated. At the point we lost her, the Duke had flown about nine hundred air miles. Her range is 1121 miles at twenty thousand feet. Flying as low as she had been and figuring the last top off of her tanks happened within 100 miles of Lenoir, our best projection of her range is this…" A map of Florida popped up, showing a rectangle. "In other words she could not fly over one hundred miles from where we lost her, or at least that is our educated guess."

"Good work Josh, and of course you too, Leon. Sometimes I forget and take your insight and foresight for granted." Jerry was serious when he said that to Leon.

"Stop it, Jerry. His ego is bigger than mine already!" He hugged Leon like they were brothers. "But you are pretty smart," Tuck smiled looking at J. Leon as he spoke.

Turning to Buddy and Billy, Josh continued, "Bringing you up to date on what happened while you were gone, most of the troops went out scouring businesses along US-321, hoping to get a glimpse of the tag number. Right now, the group is still scanning. We have a couple black Hummers so far, but they are local families, and not pickups. Let's call it a night and start fresh in the morning.

Jerry finished up, "I am thinking of sending Stella down with a couple of the crew with cameras. And, once we locate as many possible sights that we can where they could land safely, we will get some boots on the ground down there doing some real snooping." Then he addressed the guys still working, "Everyone go get some rest. Sherry has given you room keys—use them. Good night and thanks, we do appreciate every effort."

"Boss," J. Leon said after walking over to him, "I want to move a satellite down over our mystery area and do some scanning before I turn in. I think it is important and I am still sorta keyed up."

"Just do not push yourself. I know those are fine sounding words, but you know what I mean. Good night, Leon. Sherry and I are turning in."

****

Over by his computer and phone, Leon started his movement. The little satellite he was moving was dropped in space by a friend, who was an astronaut. The friend knew he had a space walk on the next mission and had told Leon to have it ready. Leon had long wanted his own satellite and was prepared to pay a rising civilian corporation three hundred thousand to take it up on one of their launches. The story was very complicated, but involved a moral debt felt by his friend for a job years earlier, involving his family.

Once the satellite was in space, J. Leon had a trained crew who sent the signals that maneuvered the 'eye' and kept records of fuel burned. He knew the formula was complicated and involved the Tsiolkosvsky rocket equation. Fuel was critical on the little softball size satellite; there was a small solar powered compressor aboard that generated the power that moved it. Tonight as he observed the terrain below change as his men moved the satellite. He felt like an astronaut, something that had once been his dream.

"Boss, that is the best we can do." It was his man Ed's voice over the phone. "You are looking at the northern quadrant that is about three quarters of the area you wanted. Tomorrow the 'eye' will have more delta-budget to expend, and we can move it deeper if necessary, but that is it for tonight."

"Thanks Ed, call it a night, I appreciate you sticking with me so late. Love to the wife and tell her I'm sorry for keeping you away."

"Okay Mary Ann, where are you, sweetheart?" Leon said to the screen as he as he moved the joystick and zoomed in on spots that looked land-able. In just a little while, Leon felt his eyes droop.

He looked at his list of ten sites and knew he did not need to continue and miss something important. He recorded his sites, put the system to sleep, and walked over to the hide-a-bed. In a few minutes, he was reclaiming energy as he slept.

Today had been a banner day for evidence, but still there were prayers, dreams and thoughts of Mary Ann. They all knew she was a tough bird, but even tough birds sometimes crash. *Hang in there, we are coming,* was in the minds of the entire search crew.

CHAPTER 11

FORMAL DINNER WITH ANDREW

She must have slept an hour, soaking in the tub, then unbidden, the thought entered her mind, *I will look like a prune.* Then sobered up—*Why in the heck do I care? I will probably die here. I wonder where I am. I doubt if anyone back home even knows I am missing.* She took some time to let her head get a little clearer for serious thinking. *Okay Mary Ann, you have toughed out a lot of things in your life, probably preparing you for this. What are you going to do? I sure do not want to be Tazered again, that is for sure.*

Just beside the tub on a beautifully accented stool lay a large towel, and as she was getting out of the tub, one of the girls mystically appeared and held the towel for her to wrap around herself. Once she was mostly dry, for the first time the young girl spoke, "I am Missie, please do take this robe," and she helped Mary Ann into the soft terry cloth rope. "Please sit here, my lady," she added, bringing her to a dressing table where Missie began to dry her hair using the same technique and blower Mary Ann always used.

This was freaking her out. *How do they know this stuff? This cannot be coincidence.* "Missie, you are very good at this, did someone teach you?"

"Yes my lady, we have been instructed and trained in the things you prefer, now I must work with this beautiful hair." Mary Ann could tell by the voice inflections, for not talk was out.

As her hair was near dry, Missie sprayed a nice

fragrance into her hair before finishing the styling. In the end, the very slight scent soothed her. And then, assisted by Missie, she was escorted to her bed—a king size bed with a canopy. "Please relax. Think about what Mr. Andrew has said and take a nap. If you want to watch a movie, here are the controls. You have nothing scheduled until dinner. That will be precisely at five fifteen. You will have assistance as you prepare. We will be starting at four fifteen; that should give you plenty of time before dinner. Thank you very much, now please relax."

"Missie, am I allowed to ask you a question without being Tazered?"

"Oh yes mistress, you can ask but first I apologize about the shock, but you must understand, Mr. Andrew is in charge here. He knows best and his word is law."

"Are you a prisoner, servant, or paid employee here?"

"Ma'am, I am here to do whatever I am told, it is my job. I follow instructions because Mr. Andrew says this is the only way the world can run, with order and discipline. Now please rest. We will return in time for dinner." Bowing, Missie backed away, turned, and left.

Well that is clear as mud… She lay back on the large canopy bed. *This is amazing, I have never been treated so well and I am a prisoner. I will cooperate and hope something happens to end this crazy nightmare. Mary Ann, you are a pretty smart chick,* she said to herself. *Who do you know that learned a foreign language during each pregnancy? Me that is who.* She recalled her pledge after Teddy Ray had said to her, you must be dumb quitting school. *I still remember thinking, I will show him, and I will show them all. I will speak Spanish before my first child is born. And I did. Then French during the second pregnancy. German was a challenge but I mastered conversational German on the last pregnancy. That was when hubby said, 'That is it. No more kids and no more languages, already I don't know for sure if you are cursing me or not,' and he laughed.*

So many thoughts crossed her mind, but she remembered Andrew saying he was protecting his investment. *I know it must have cost a lot to arrange all this, but why? What kind of investment am I? At seventy years old, I am definitely not arm candy for some young stud. Old men would buy a young girl, wouldn't they?*

Okay, this is what he said: I am going to have riches, servants, and so on. Can't I just act the part and wait for a chance to pass a note or letter, or even phone home or the police? That is surely better than getting hit with the Tazer. I am smart enough to read in between the lines. He will drug me if I do not cooperate, and I do not want to be a drug addict. I have known a couple, no way. Oh, Dusty, Buck, come and find me. What am I messed up in? She actually drifted off to sleep ... thinking...

"Mrs. LaRoach, Mary, it is time to prepare for dinner." She awoke to the smiling faces of two girls, Missie and Mae. "Time to get dressed. Your underwear is here, we will step to the side as you slip into them." They turned discreetly.

I shouldn't be surprised that the new clothes fit, she thought.

Mae approached with a beautiful evening dress. "You will be beautiful in this, my lady." The pampering continued, and she was escorted to the dressing table, where make up was laid out. Mae started her makeup. *These girls are professionals; I am getting a complete makeover like on TV.* When the makeup was finished, Millie again worked on her hair. The results were amazing.

Next came some nice matching jewelry, then dark hosiery and matching half heels. Finally, it was time for dinner. They escorted her down. As they neared the first floor, Mae called out, "Ms. Mary LaRoach for dinner." Andrew stepped to the bottom of the stairs, wearing suit and tie. "Ah, Madam, you look fantastic this evening. He bowed, and then offered his arm. Following his lead, Mary Ann slipped her arm through and they moved to the table. Gentlemanly, Andrew seated Mary Ann. After ensuring she was comfortable, he moved to a chair opposite her.

The meal consisted of turkey, deliciously prepared with great vegetables. There was very little chit chat but Mary Ann was learning by observing. She had lived her life (after a few false starts) by observing situations and anticipating the various responses to the obvious answers, choosing the best for her and her family before giving a response. As the dinner progressed, she noticed the cook and the two girls were the entire visible staff. What disturbed her most, even more than her own present situation, was the fact her mind was telling her: *These people are scared to death of this man. They are not employees; they are prisoners just like I am.*

The dessert was the best blueberry cheesecake she had ever eaten served with the delicious coffee. Andrew was correct; it was the best coffee she had ever enjoyed.

"Missie, we will have coffee on the portico, please. Ms. LaRoach and I will chat and enjoy the evening air. Come, Mary." He took her hand very gently and guided her through the beautifully designed doors to the outside. As coffee was being served, Andrew asked, "Was dinner satisfactory, Mary?"

"Yes of course, it was delicious. If I were your guest for the week, I would be more than thrilled."

"Now, please listen, Mary, this is no game. This is life and death for you. I know you will take this personally, but you shouldn't. I am a business man. I am known in many parts of the world as a man who can and will supply anything, at the right price. The men who contact me are wealthy, the top one percent of the world. Unfortunately, some want sex toys or sex slaves and for a price I supply them. Now, as you listen, you are thinking, *disgusting.* I understand that; it is the way of your culture, or 'your raising', as you would say. However, from my world, it is business and life. Before you respond and ask, your selection has nothing to do with sex."

"You are right. That does sound disgusting, and scary. Don't you have any feelings for girls or women, even me? Humans are not a commodity on a shelf in a store. We are real and have feelings, plans, and desires. We have family. Do you have family, Andrew?"

"You are wrong, Mary. Humans are commodities. Humans have been collected and sold since the beginning of man. Your own country is proof of that; you know it for a fact. It has never stopped. Many Americans are still slaves to the state. Besides that, you are a very religious woman. Ever look at the lives of people in what you call your Old Bible? Folks were sold and slaved thousands of years ago. It is and always has been a business, just like prostitution."

"Since you are familiar with my religion, you know that Jesus came to change that and let us live by faith. We were to be free."

"So, how is that working out for you right now?"

"Oh Andrew, it isn't over. We just met."

"Oh yes, it is over for you. You really do not know it yet; it will take a couple weeks for that to become a reality in your mind, but it will happen. To modify a phrase so popular among you Christians, Andrew never fails. After a couple of weeks you will receive specialized training for a week or so, and then you will be delivered to the man who has purchased you. You are going to be a source of pride for him. You will be treated like a queen. Mary, you do not know it but you are one fortunate lady."

"You are telling me, some person is paying you a lot of money for an old woman?"

"Oh Mary, sweetheart, your price tag would astound you. However, your value drops if I must modify your mind. I do not want to lose value, so that is why I will first try the method that gives the most profit, of course."

"You said, men from all over the world contact you. This foolish man who wants an old woman, where is he from?"

"Within two weeks you will not only know where, but you will see videos. You will be so pleased Mary; this man is not only wealthy but handsome."

"Is there anything I can do to change your mind or the course of action?"

"Absolutely nothing will interfere with this transaction. Now I want to be honest with you; as a business man, that is the safest path. Mary Ann Kirkman is dead. She will never live again. You can spend a day crying over her, but I will not allow more. I want you to know that I know you will plan to 'play along with Andrew's plan' because you do not want another shock. You also think there will come a time when you can pass a letter or message to your grieving family and someone will come and save you. You look around at my employees here and think they are in the same boat as you are; you have observed correctly. You have even thought of asking them for help. Believe me, they are not about to help someone they do not know. How am I doing?"

"Fairly accurate." *Fairly ... heck, you have read me perfectly, so I will change some tactic.*

"I want you to know that your life is valuable to me, so I will not break any bones or scar you. I know you like Missie and Mae, they are sweet and cooperative, but they will never help you. Do you know how I can be so sure of them?"

Because they do not want to be tazed, and I can understand that.

"There is your simplistic western breeding coming out, if either girl would tell or breathe something, whisper it or write it and pass it … if they would help you in any way other than I direct, I would kill them." Mary Ann gasped involuntarily, then Andrew continued, "Before they're killed, they would be given to my men to enjoy as sex toys for a couple of days, then they would bring them to me and I would kill them. Unlike you, my dear Mary, they are only a lower grade commodity; they are not important. I can replace them in a day. You may ask, how do they know this? Because, my innocent Mary, they have seen it done so they know without a doubt what will happen if they assist anyone against my word."

"I have never known anyone as despicable as you. How can you talk of killing someone like you were stepping on a cockroach?"

"Oh Mary, you see, I was not raised with your weird 'Christian' values. We laugh at your naiveté;

your double standards. Christians kill from a distance, so they do not see blood. A rocket or a drone flown into a building to kill a man, what your government does not tell you is they killed his wife and three children as well. I have heard Christians say that all Muslims should be killed. As they said it, I believed they would do it, if possible. Oh, and to answer your mental question, no, I am not a Muslim. Their beliefs are as silly as the Christians'. I do have some Islamic background, but I have no religion other than business. If I kill someone, they are gone forever. The Muslim and the Christian think they have a paradise or heaven they go to when they die. What childish silliness. What you think of me does not matter. I do whatever it takes to deliver a product as ordered. And you, my dear, are a beautiful product. Now, do you have any more questions?"

"Naturally, I would like to know what I am worth, as your commodity."

"That is a fair question, my dear. If you are delivered as sweet and beautiful as you are tonight, you are worth one and a half million American dollars. Putting it plainly, if you are a drug addict, you are only worth nine hundred thousand. So I would appreciate it if you did not force me to use the needles."

"Now just a question, since neither I nor my family has ever even thought of that kind of money, and since they will never see me again…" Tears formed unbidden in Mary Ann's eyes. "…And you get the full price for me—would you agree to give each of my kids eighty thousand dollars?"

Laughing, Andrew was taken by surprise. "Lady, you are a wonder. I have never had anyone try to bargain with me. Let me think on that and give you the answer over breakfast. Now it is time I think for us both to retire." He rose and gave Mary Ann his hand and walked her to the stairway where Missie and Mae were waiting. "I have chosen wisely, Mary. Sleep well."

Inside the room, she found fresh fruit and some fresh orange juice. "My lady, if you need something to help you sleep, here is a mild sleep aid that Andrew has authorized. He recommended the movie. All you need to do is touch the power button and the movie will play. It will turn itself off at the end. Your night clothes are laid out. Would you like assistance in preparing for bed?"

Making her funny face, she saw the first glint of a smile, then said in her mock western voice, "Naw, pardners, I can handle it. Been used to putting this old horse to bed for many years now." Both girls giggled and left.

Mary Ann needed time to pray and think. *Ah, I must listen. Listen because I have felt that there were times in my life that I was directed to do something, but that was in situations when someone might be needing an Afghan or just to make someone feel better or even fixing someone a meal.*

Now girl, this one is serious. Okay now, what am I going to do? I am in the hands of a cold-blooded killer with nice manners. Is that weird or what? Her mind played over how nonchalantly he had said, 'I will kill', and then his mention that the girls are a low value commodity. *Wow, now was I serious about the money for the kids? Funny, I don't even know what drove me to say that? I have no idea. BUT if this whole thing plays out, my kids should get something.*

And then she cried. And she cried some more. And then she thought, *He said Mary Ann Kirkman is dead. Well, that is what you think Mr. Andrew. I am not dead by a long shot.* She covered her head with the sheets. No one was going to read her body language or whatever they did. It seemed a lifetime ago, but just the previous day she'd been happy on top of a mountain in North Carolina, Her last thought as she drifted off was: *Mary Ann is ALIVE!*

CHAPTER 12

RECONNASENCE MVA STYLE

Tuesday

"Okay folks, it is Tuesday morning. Mary Ann disappeared one and a half days ago. We have made a lot of progress, but now it is time to get down to brass tacks. Trails get old and witnesses forget." Jerry was talking to his crew along with Buck, Dusty, two FBI agents and one deputy Sherriff. Some were looking over their notes, others glancing at some search on their laptops, while J. Leon, who had grabbed a couple hours sleep, was back on the screen looking for landing spots.

J. Leon took the lead. "For you that do not know, I am most sure we have tracked the plane to near south central Florida. There is where the plane dropped so low, the FAA radar lost it. We have a suspected area of terminus for the flight. It is pretty large and I am looking. What we need is all possible landing sites in the area I have marked here." Leon pointed to the screen. "You can get the geo-coordinates from off the screen. We need some strong possibilities so we can check them out. Our satellite in this area will be fueled up enough to move again in two hours. I just about exhausted the little dude's fuel last night."

"I suggest using Google Maps, or any of the several maps that will identify the homes, businesses and ranches. You can get the names off the County tax records. Just because a ranch looks legit, we know it may not be. But at first let's give those the benefit of a doubt, and go for the questionable ones. That is just my opinion."

Again Jerry took over, "Stella, you and Vickie need to have the bird ready to go down and check the area out. Besides the bird's recon camera, we have some good handheld cameras. Two of the guys can go and bring back some reconnaissance photos for us to look at. I know it is a dream, but I would like for the recalled MVA and volunteer associates to have Mary Ann safe before Tuesday afternoon, or at the latest, Wednesday evening. I know that is asking a lot, but we have no idea what the crook's plans are. We hope she stays in Florida, but we do not know that for sure."

"I would like to hear some more ideas on why Mary Ann was targeted. Common sense tells us this is no random act. No one has been contacted about ransom. Agents Mix and Taft can help us more than anyone here. I know you put a lot of stuff out yesterday on this subject. Anything you can add?"

"Well, Buddy came back with the idea of body parts. That possibility would be on the long list, but not a short one. Some speculation here, keep that in mind. We have had hints that there are elite specialty groups out there that will get you anything or anybody, for the right price. In a stretch, this could be a possibility; I would list it far above body parts. And to clarify, I understand the body parts idea was mentioned to get us looking from another position. That is good," Mix related as she sipped her coffee.

"Okay, thinking that direction for a minute— seniors are special, but we must consider the value versus cost. Now, looking at this operation, what would an elite group have to charge to make this profitable? What would justify someone paying MEGA bucks for such a venture? What would just the basic costs be to the supplier?"

Taft spoke up—"Figures are my specialty Jerry, if this action is coming out of south Florida and back. Cost alone would be about fifteen thousand for logistics involved in Florida and North Carolina. Our research would show that the pilot was paid twenty to thirty Thousand to put his face on a camera and rent the plane. His flying helper would be paid ten thousand. That would be close to fifty to sixty thousand. Normally, the planning and lesser workers would be two thousand a day, and considering on the outside ten bodies, that would be twenty thousand more. Totaling less than a hundred thousand … if this situation here were totally an FBI action, and not yours, we would calculate total cost of workers and hardware to one hundred thousand dollars."

"What about the chain of command?"

"Rule of thumb, we triple the bottom layer cost, or four hundred thousand. Therefore the subject would have to be worth very close to one million dollars."

Jerry was standing, staring into space chewing on his pen. "Now folks, I would give a million dollars for my mama or my wife, but would I give a million dollars for a substitute, one seventy years old?"

"Would a man who was in love with his wife, and very wealthy, seek to buy a replacement if the present wife passed away?" threw in Rankin.

"It is too much of a variable, but I will throw it in anyway, an old man who is mentally challenged might do just that," Mix said.

"Now, from another angle, what if it is not the mentally disturbed man wanting the wife back, but a greedy corporate board that wants things signed over to them and the man's wife had always been his cane to lean on for tough decisions?" Taft added.

"But in those cases, wouldn't they just hire an actress and apply enough make up to get the desired results?" Sherry questioned, finally getting involved in this discussion.

"Okay, just for a follow up, let's do a little

searching on billionaires and loss of loved ones. Better yet, search for a billionaire who has lost a female companion," Jerry suggested.

"Pay dirt!" The yell came from Megan, Josh's new wife who was on leave from her job at the hospital and helping review the many security tapes they had rounded up from businesses along highway 321. She was a little embarrassed when she realized how loud she had yelled. She had frozen an image of a vehicle tag on his screen. Everyone gathered around her. "Florida license tag number 531-B32 on a big fat black Hummer, BoJangles drive-thru, about ten minutes after we estimate the aircraft flew south. Yippee!"

"Okay, who owns it?" Jerry asked.

"I'm on it." Josh said as he hugged Megan tight and they shared a kiss. Of course the cat calls came but they were short this time. Josh sat down at his large computer smiling and started hitting keys.

Mix was looking over his shoulder. "Isn't that illegal, my friend?"

"Nah, it is just a short cut. I could get the information if I called the Florida DMV directly.

This is public information." Josh smiled as he keyed into the system.

"Of course you are right. Hundreds of times I wish I could have done the same, but if I had gotten any evidence, it would have been inadmissible in court."

"That is the point. I am not looking for evidence to take to court. I am looking to save a lady's life if at all possible," Josh retorted, smiling. Megan, who was observing, cracked a smile, too. This happened to be her first 'event' since she and Josh got married.

Seeing Megan's expression, Sherry moved to her side. "Yes, you have a right to smile and be proud. He tells us that your fellow workers say you are one of the best on the floor at Presbyterian. Well, let me tell you, your man is one of the best at what he does, maybe even THE BEST. I have been privileged to watch him in action. There was a time when I needed the MVA, he was right in the middle, and I am alive. Oh yes, you have a right to smile."

They hugged. "I'll tell you this, Megan, I would be a complete wreck if I knew Mary Ann was missing and I did not have these guys to rely on. I would hate to be the … misguided thugs that have done this. They will be located and dealt with harshly and then her family will have their mother back and I will continue to enjoy a great friend."

Sherry saw the door open. Stephen gave her the *shhh* signal as he and Jenn came in the door, closing it quietly. Stephen walked over to Jerry. "So what do you need, boss?"

Jerry was startled a little but tried not show it. "I would ask you how you got in through a locked door, but that would be stupid." He grabbed Stephen in a bear hug. Seeing Jennifer, a bigger smile came on his face, and he immediately embraced her. "Thanks for coming guys; mill around and I am sure you will find a spot. Jennifer, it is great to see you, and we are glad you brought Stephen along."

"I didn't give the man much choice. It was let me come along or I would pitch a hissy fit. Reece said to tell you if you really needed an expert, she could get off from work." Jennifer spoke with a sly smile.

Sherry and Megan took Jennifer to the side to tell her the latest. "Can you guys stay the night?" Sherry asked.

"Oh yeah, Stephen was going buggy to be with the crew."

"Okay, let's take a walk and get you a room, the more the merrier in this case. They need every bit of help they can get, even from us bystanders."

The motel manager was glad and asked if there were more to come. Then the girls walked back towards the Command area, Jennifer still being brought up to date.

The Hummer was registered to the 'Andrew Care Consultants', a not for profit corporation. It was properly registered. Having a list of addresses for the Corporation Primaries, the search continued. The simple thing was to use Google Earth to look at the addresses listed for the registration and the corporation; all empty lots, according to Google. The address on the registration for the Hummer was a PMB mail box in a strip mall.

The PMB stood for 'Personal Mail Box'. The actual address proved to be a Pack and Ship Mail forwarding service, found by Matt by simply using the zip code. This helped; it was located in Arcadia,

Florida, but that was no guarantee that the owners lived there or even near. The owner of a PMB could be in Dallas, Texas and get their mail at the PMB. They retrieved their mail by calling for it to be forwarded to another address normally. That process of receiving mail is used by many transits.

The PMB address being in Arcadia was in the projected area for landing sites. East of Arcadia stood hundreds of square miles of open land. The area is very sparsely populated all the way to Lake Okeechobee and the home of many ranches and orange groves.

"Okay troops, let's compile the list and get this reconnaissance plane in the air. I have changed my mind, gather around. I am looking at a very small possibility, but consider this: what if you actually saw an aircraft, say the Duke, with a new paint job and Mary Ann being loaded on board? What could Stella and two camera men do? My answer is, not much. So I want at least two other guys besides Buddy and Tuck on the flight. I want chutes and silenced weapons, flash bangs, whatever you guys figure you might need. I am saying if an opportunity avails itself, I want the MVA to be ready."

"I'm with you, Jerry," Buddy said. "I can have the stuff we need at the Gastonia Airport in an hour. Stella can drop us in to pick it up. Gastonia is faster and less traffic than Charlotte."

"Go for it. Now if there are no objections, I think—"

"Jerry," Dusty interrupted. "I want to go. I have logged fifty-three jumps in the airborne and a few sky diving. If there is a chance, I want to be there."

"Dusty, I am going to rely on your professionalism as a LEO. Tuck will be in charge as far as 'orders' go and I expect you to follow them. I am a little reluctant because it is your mother and you might allow your training to be overridden by personal feelings. On the other hand, I do not blame you for wanting to be there, so I am okay with it. Stephen, you will suit up also, a present since you just arrived." The rest were disappointed, Jerry could tell. "I do not think anything will come of this flight except photos. I need folk here thinking and looking at film as it comes in over the net."

"Got you chief, but I really did want a vacation to Florida." Matt laughed.

"Okay, take the list. Keep in touch. Grab some fruit and a sandwich and get ready to head south," Jerry said. "It is still a good ways to noon. This should keep us in the game, but pray that we find that landing site. We need it."

"Jerry, I just talked to my guys. They will have the stuff at Gastonia, no problem," Buddy explained.

Jennifer and Stephen embraced and the rest of the crew gave the normal cat calls and cute statements. "Jealousy is beneath you guys … I thought," was Stephen's comeback.

"Jerry, my guy just said Mark David was there and ready if you have room, Mary Ann is one of his favorite people," Buddy called out.

"Tell him we will be glad to have him aboard." Jerry smiled and gave the thumbs up. He remembered Mark David back in the time he was wandering the streets of Mt. Bell as Rags. It was easy to respect the man.

This was an exciting time; it always was. Everyone felt the electricity in the air. They all wanted to head to Florida. There was a feeling something was going to happen. "I feel good about this," Jerry said. "Mary Ann has no way of knowing what is happening up here in Lenoir, so a few prayers would be in order. We cannot contact her, but maybe the Lord will help and deliver a message."

Sherry smiled. She was proud of her Jerry, and his acceptance of Divine leadership. When they renewed their acquaintance after her husband's death, there was an honest doubt in Jerry's mind about any Divine Power. Seeing the change over the years had been wonderful. The deep changes had started during that terrible time of her kidnapping. It had been a thrill to her since she *knew*, she was one of God's favorites. She said that often because of all the good things that had happened since she married Jerry.

CHAPTER 13

TUESDAY MORNING IN FLORIDA

Mary Ann was awakened by a soft knock on the door. "Yes, who is it?"

"It is only Missie, Mistress Mary."

"Come in, child." Mary Ann was climbing out of bed as Missie arrived with a hot cup of coffee and a chilled glass of Orange Juice.

"Well, how thoughtful my dear, thank you."

"It was Andrew's orders, Mistress. I only do as he bids."

"Well it is sweet anyway, thank you again."

Every word these girls speak is recorded and they know it. One wrong word and they would die. What a terrible life. For seventy years, I have been so blessed and didn't know it. I have never been under a threat of immediate death. I cannot begin to imagine the stress level of these girls, really of everyone in this house.

"Please Mistress, wash your face and do your requirements in the toilet, and I will prepare you for the day."

Entering the bathroom, Mary Ann realized it had only been two days since she was safe, or thought she was safe at home. Here she found her life beginning to be programmed and scheduled, out of her control. Then she smiled to herself. *No Andrew, it is not going to work. Somehow he seems to know exactly what I plan and think. Now that means I have to do like I heard once, 'Think outside the box'; something he does not suspect or anticipate.* Her toilet rituals were performed automatically as she thought. Walking out, she found Missie at the dressing table with make-up and necessities ready and waiting. *I guess, if that is what a person has wanted in life, this would be easy to get used to. But to an independent person like I have been all my life, this is okay for the 'yearly splurge' but every day, it just isn't me.*

"A touch of blue eye shadow today, and more rouge," Missie said as she worked steadily. Mary Ann was amazed as a transformation occurred before her very eyes. "Now, we will do a small modification to the hair style, and you can be a younger lady today." Missie actually smiled and winked.

"You do a beautiful job my sweet, but my heart is not in being younger, just somewhere else."

"Oh not to worry, my lady; we all feel that way at first but when you realize it is your fate, and life is meant to be lived no matter where you are, things get much easier." Missie smiled again, this time raising her eyebrows a little, causing Mary Ann to wonder but not ask.

She was told to put on another dress, much simpler than the one she'd worn the previous evening, but still elegant with matching flats for her feet. She admired herself in the mirror. *If necessary, can I use violence? If I am forced to, could I actually kill a human? I know I could never take a life in as cavalier a manner as Andrew does, but could I do it to save myself and somehow get back to my family?* Unbidden, the thought of one of her last Bible readings in Judges came to mind. *I know I had read it before, but now as nasty as it was, it comes to mind.* She remembered being appalled when a man named Ehud tricked the very fat King then stabbed him with a short sword so deep; he lost the handle in his fat belly. *He did this to save his people. Then later on judges a woman who, to save her people, had driven a tent stake through a man's head. Could I do that?*

"Mistress, are you here?" It was Missie smiling and breaking her away from her thoughts.

"Oh yes, I was just thinking of a book I read. I am ready."

The same ritual was followed; she was met at the base of the stairs by Andrew and escorted to breakfast. Soon they were seated and started to eat. "My dear Mary," Andrew said. "I have given some thought to your request concerning a monetary gift to your children. I am inclined to make a *deal* with you. If you give up the silly thought of what you consider *escape*, and cooperate completely in your reprogramming, you have my word I will give your children the compensation you suggest. Believe me; I have never considered such a thing. But you, Mary, are an exceptional person. Down deep, I think I feel a little regret for denying you to your family."

"Now Andrew, I will be honest, I have no idea why I mentioned that, so please give me a day to reach a mental satisfaction that I have done something for my kids. This is all surreal, surely you understand that."

"Certainly my dear, you have brought some variety into my life that I have not expected. I think I am respecting you more as this arrangement progresses. You are indeed special, Mary LaRoach."

After the breakfast, which was very tasty and filling, they again had coffee outside. "I think we will take a walk later this morning. Being a mountain lady, you need to get used to the flat country. It is very beautiful in its own way."

"I have never been bought or sold, so I would like to know the procedure. If I do agree that Mary Ann is dead, do you deliver me gift wrapped, or does my new owner come and pick me up?"

"Please, you must understand, Mary," Andrew said sternly, "it is not if you agree, because the end result will be the same. We do not use the terms sold and bought; they are too basic. They do not convey the truth of the arrangement. This is business, pure and simple. A commodity, *you*, will be delivered by me in good or excellent condition, which depends on you by the way, whether you agree or not."

"Well, I must tell you Andrew, it is hard to wrap my mind around business deals involving selling human beings."

"Oh I understand completely, Mary. I am very familiar with the silly western idea that a woman is anything more than a vessel to bring more men into the world. I am not narrow minded enough to think that there can be no enjoyment to the female, there definitely can be, but she must recognize she is only here to bear children and to satisfy the desires of man. In doing so, she can be allowed certain leeway in that respect." He paused a moment to give her a look of pity. "You, my dear, are past child bearing, past the time you were put here for. But in this world we have men who have been changed by age who start thinking in western terms of love. That is where you, a beautiful, tall, slender beauty in her seventies, come into the picture. A very nice but foolishly rich man has asked me to deliver a lady like you to him, and that is what I will do."

Mary Ann was honestly trying to understand all this but remained dumbfounded. This was like something out of a science fiction movie. It proved hard for her to digest this concept.

"I said you are past child bearing, but you can still be a joy to a man. This man who is willing to pay over a million dollars for a lady that will make him happy, honor him, and satisfy him is seeking that joy. He is willing to give you a life of the 'rich and famous', as you Americans are so prone to say, just for you to share his life. This is one of the few business agreements in which the 'victim', as you now see yourself, is going to be rewarded more than they could ever have dreamed. Logic alone should tell you that you are one lucky woman."

"It all sounds fine the way you say it, but it is hard to see myself as just a toy, a plaything at the beck and call of a man."

"I am amazed at the Christian ignorance. Even in your Holy Book, God created the woman for the man, did he not? And all through that Book, woman is bought. But believe me, Mary, you are not here to make any decision, I will make them for you as the man is destined to do, because we are stronger and superior. It is the way of the world. So believe me, in two weeks, lady, you will know this and it will be a part of you. You see, I know your life, Mary; you and all women have always been controlled by a man."

"I think I told you, Andrew; I have been taught that Jesus came to change some of that attitude." Mary Ann spoke a little more harshly than she meant.

"At times, throughout the ages, there have been women who believed that. Consider the Muslim; he will beat a woman who has the audacity to think that she is more than she is. The western man is different; he is a mole, no guts, no power. Some cry and others just get a divorce because they are not men enough to control a silly woman. Me? I know who is the master. In this world, I take what I want. You are a very interesting subject, Mary, but still, when the chips are down, please for your sake, remember it is not personal—it is business."

Not knowing what to say, Mary Ann just sat quietly, sipping coffee. *Maybe I could kill you. You are an arrogant son of a dog. I really do need a plan.*

"Now, Mary LaRoach, I have work to do. In the meantime, take a stroll. One or both of the girls will accompany you. Enjoy the hospitality here. Get used to the opulence, for compared to where you are going, this place would be a dog house. You do not know it yet, but I am doing you a favor and being paid handsomely for it."

Andrew escorted her inside and turned her over to her 'handlers'.

The girls took the lead and they started their walk outside. The ranch seemed to be huge. The girls told her that the entire Ranchero was surrounded by an electric fence. They had heard that there was a place in the hacienda where the fence and grounds were monitored on TV screens. The land was unlike any she had known. She spotted a few groves of trees in the distance. Cattle grazed on the low grass. It was not desert land but it was very flat, having only a few rises in the distance. As Mary Ann gazed out in that direction, oh how she longed to see some of her family driving up. In spite of herself, she found herself tearing up. She felt a soft facial towel being slipped into her hand. Deep down inside, she knew these girls would like to walk out of here also.

"You girls must have been here a long time. Are there many visitors like myself here at the ranch?" Mary Ann tried to sound casual.

"We are so glad to have you here, Mistress. Andrew says you are a special guest. There are things we will not talk about. All people are destined to serve someone; at present we choose to serve Master Andrew, and he is good to us."

"Can you tell me where I am, what country? Am I still in the United States?"

"Oh, we find that information is not important. The food is good. We have water and a nice place to sleep. What else does the person need?"

They came upon a beautiful little stream, its water clear and inviting. The stream was wide in spots and also very narrow in others; narrow enough to step over. The banks were steep on either side, showing the stream had cut its way down through the soft sand over the years. The banks of the creek were only three or four feet high in most places. The area where they were standing, the water touched the land like the sea on a beach. Palms and Palmettos followed the creek as far as you could see. There was one road coming into the ranch, and several buildings.

They sat in a swing under a shade that was built to hold the swing, and covered by palm limbs. Everything seemed so tropical. In the distance, she could see the runway and barn type hangar where she had first stepped from the plane. Near the hangar, she spotted several men around a blue and white airplane.

The three sat and chatted about the nice weather and cool water. Nothing of substance could be drawn from the girls. She noticed every once in a while they would glance up. Mary Ann knew they were being observed, even here.

At last, Missie looked at her watch. "It is time to return to the hacienda. Food will be served in half an hour. You want to be ready to meet Andrew for a nice lunch."

Mary Ann smiled. *I can think of a million things I would rather do, ladies.*

As they walked into the house, Mary Ann heard an airplane engine start. The thought came to her mind: *Going after someone else to give me company.* Then immediately the engine stopped. *Well, I guess I get no company. I guess they are just working on it.*

CHAPTER 14

ABOUT CATCHING TWO RATS

The plane was ready when the reconnaissance crew reached the airport. On the flight to Gastonia, Dusty became better acquainted with the others. They also filled him in on Mark David, who would join them. The plane would be about at capacity with the essential baggage and five passengers.

Gastonia was a very fast turnaround since there is very little traffic. They were soon on their way and Stella pushed the throttle to max. The little plane was pushing five hundred miles per hour.

The MVA had always prided itself in fast reaction. They were approaching the search area just past noon. Tuck sat in the jump seat, calling out coordinates of possible sights. They were looking for a Duke aircraft, a black Hummer pickup, and men of different sizes. Everyone had pictures. All individuals near the runways were to be photographed. Every once in a while, someone would call out, 'Lock' and Tuck would punch the GPS to record the coordinates. Everyone would have liked to be at a lower elevation, but from experience, they knew they needed to be above three thousand feet. No one wanted their flight to appear to be searching.

After two hours of eye strain and about a fourth of the area covered, they had only spotted a couple of possible landing strips; they appeared to be small operational strips for crop-dusters and such, so they did not look very promising. Mark David called 'lock', and then said, "Everyone look at about two o'clock. Eyes were peeled as they were crossing, and

Stella throttled back on instinct. "This looks good. What do you guys think?"

"Got a house and a barn type hangar," Stephen chimed in.

"It appears to be a big cattle ranch," Tuck called from upfront. Do you see any people?"

In a few seconds, they would be past the site. "Oh ho, at the edge of the barn, is that a black truck?" piped in Dusty.

"I think you were right, Dusty. Steady as she goes, Stella I want to plug this camera into the laptop and blow up some shots." Buddy looked at the blow ups. Disappointed, he then added, "Negative, guys, that is a big Chevy in the barn. But it is still the best site so far in my estimation."

They continued the search. At about 3:30, Tuck spoke over the intercom, "What do we have here? Dead ahead, guys."

Stella veered off a little so everyone could view out the starboard windows. Cameras were going and Stella had engaged the plane's recon camera.

"Looks like an airplane with a shiny new paint

job, nice blue and white."

"That also looks like a Duke, doesn't it?" They saw a Barn suitable for a hangar and a large home a few hundred yards away. Lots of Black Angus cattle were grazing in the green fields. "I see three men; they should produce some good pictures," Buddy said.

"Stella I think Arcadia is close to here. They should have a place to land. I think everyone needs a break, including you," Tuck said, smiling. "And I think we might have something."

"Recovering her clipboard, Stella looked it over. "Yeah that is the home of strip X06, plenty of room and they even have a tower of sorts." Stella adjusted her course.

"Okay crew, we are going down for a little while. Stella is taking us to the vacation town of Arcadia, Florida. It is the home of wild nightlife and twenty four hour bars." Tuck laughed.

"Buddy was setting up his lap top for more film images."

In five minutes, Stella announced, "We will be landing in four minutes, please buckle up and get ready. I am not sure of the run surface." The runway turned out to be a very good asphalt runway and they taxied to the visiting planes' staging area. She cut the engines. "I have to go inside. The batteries will give enough power for a while. We might find a meeting place inside. Come on with me, Tuck. You can check on that while I take care of flying business."

The terminal was very informal as most private ports were. Andrea, the only guy in the office on duty, gladly took the credit card for port usage and the fuel. He called the local fuel truck and, just as they found the room they could use, the truck pulled up to the plane. Stella liked to be present for the fueling so she went out to the plane and gave directions to the room and every one deplaned as required by FAA. She was very protective of her bird and would stay with the craft until all fueling was done, then she would check the engines before going back inside.

Inside, Buddy had already loaded everyone's camera cards into the laptop. When everyone was assembled, he started the show, moving very slow and zooming in on any particular point someone would suggest. The plane at the last ranch was a

Duke alright; they were even sure it was their object that had been repainted, but everyone readily admitted they could be wrong. They zoomed on one small guy. "Hey, this little guy has a red ball cap; the old dude did say a small guy with a red ball cap as he was describing the guy that escorted Mary Ann from the Hummer to the plane in Lenoir, didn't he?" In just a few minutes, Buddy was sending all the camera shots back to the command post in Lenoir. "We will see what Melvin has to say; it may take a half an hour to get him back down to the motel."

Tuck was on the phone to Jerry to inform him of the download coming, and to let him know they did have one good suspect sight. Of course, the guys that were left in Lenoir would be scouring the pictures with magnifying glasses to look for points of intelligence.

While Tuck was filling Jerry in on the flight, the others were busy thinking of the best way to make sure the site they were interested in was the one. While they were talking, a prop job landed and Stephen looked out the window. "Well, look what we have here." Everyone gathered around the window. "It would appear that luck is with us. Am I seeing the same white and blue Duke we saw from the air not thirty minutes ago?"

"You guys stick here and be ready to take that crew if necessary," Buddy said. "We want them alive and well. They could be our guys," and he went out the door.

"Jerry, something just came up. Talk later." Tuck followed Buddy out the door.

"Andrea, my man," Buddy called. "Do you know that plane that just came in?"

"I think it is the new one Andrew of the 'Conestoga Ranch' just bought. Hoss called and said they needed to fuel their new plane up."

By this time, the crew was climbing out of the plane. "So you know the crew."

"Sure, we call them Hoss and Little Joe. They are regulars."

Buddy and Tuck pulled their 'Courtesy FBI shields'. "Andrea," Buddy said, "Do not call the local police yet, but be ready to do just that. We are going to take Hoss and Little Joe into that room we are renting for a talk. It may be nothing and we hope it is not, just be cool, okay?"

"S-sure FBI, I have never been in trouble."

"Well, you are certainly not in trouble now either. By the way, do they ever bring anyone else with them when they fly in?"

"They bring Drey and Craig at times. I think they are the cowboys."

Back in the room, Tuck said, "You guys wander outside, you know the drill."

Tuck then walked outside with Buddy, over to the plane where 'Little Joe' had a rag and was wiping some oil off the cowling. "Hey man, nice Duke you have here. How does she handle?" He intentionally walked over to the man like he thought he was the pilot.

"How the hell would he know? He can't fly a kite," Hoss cut in.

"Hey, my man, you must be Hoss. Does she handle well? She looks brand new."

Tuck was checking the paint; it was obviously fresh. "Hey, get away from the plane, man!" Hoss yelled at Tuck, who held up his hands in surrender.

"Just admiring it. I didn't know you were so touchy." Buddy stood beside Little Joe and Tuck walked over to Hoss. "We could use your help. Last night a small plane went down near here. We suspected it was loaded with drugs. Have you heard or seen anything of a wreckage?" As he said that, he flipped his badge out for Hoss to see and Buddy did the same.

Hoss looked decidedly less confrontational now. "Sorry about the yelling, but we have to keep this bird ready for the boss. But about a downed bird, no I haven't seen a thing. This is pretty far inland for stuff like that."

"Yeah, but the crooks are getting braver about flying further in, before giving it to their mules. Could you guys come inside? I am sure you know Andrea; we just need your names on our report. You know the government, you gotta fill in all the blanks, and half our time is spent doing the stupid paperwork," Tuck said disgustingly, and started walking back to the office. Hoss followed, with Buddy and Little Joe behind making small talk.

"Do Hoss and you round up cows with an airplane? Andrea said you guys were ranchers."

"No man, the boss have cowboys for that. We just fly the boss around. He is an important guy," Little Joe said proudly.

"I fly the boss around," Hoss said over his shoulder. They were up the steps and on the porch and through the door, still talking.

"I never met a rancher with a plane before," Tuck said as he led Hoss past Andrea. "We will be right back out, Andrea. Thanks for the use of the room."

Dusty and Stephen were back in the room first, Mark David was going to be bringing up the rear, to be the last person in the room. After both men were inside, they were facing handguns with silencers. Little Joe was pushed to the side, and faster than expected, Hoss parried the handgun with his forearm and headed for the door. Standing in the door, Mark David hit him in the midsection with everything he had and Hoss bent double before he made the door. Using his right knee, Mark finished the job as he raised it like lightning and brought it up into his face. Hoss fell to the floor like a concrete slab.

"Cuff both of them and also use the Gorilla

tape."

"Stephen, you and Mark David go out and look over the Duke, get the serial numbers of the fuselage and engines. I will get Jerry on the line." While Tuck was calling, he looked over to see that both Hoss and Little Joe were trussed up. "Yeah Boss, I am sorry for the interruption, but we now have in our fat little hands a couple of guys called Hoss and Little Joe. ... Yes, you heard right, now guess what type of plane they just flew into the airport at Arcadia?"

"No wonder you are the boss, you got that right away. What I need is the serial numbers of the engines and fuselage of the Duke. ... I will be waiting for your call."

As he talked, Hoss had came around, but was playing possum. Little Joe had been listening intently and obviously looking a little scared.

"Dusty, have you used that Tazer you have on your belt lately?"

"No sir, but I am beginning to want to."

The room went quiet, with only a couple keyboards clicking, and the sound of breathing.

After about five minutes, the two guys came back in with some information. "Here are the serial numbers. They look genuine." From his position on the floor, Hoss smiled a little. "But Stephen found a couple of maps." The phone rang and Tuck held his hand up for silence as he answered. At the same time Buddy was looking at his phone, he received the serial numbers in a text.

"Yeah boss, evidently Buddy just got them on his phone. Hang on, I will let you listen."

"The serial numbers actually on the engines and fuselage are not the same as those on the stolen Duke." Hoss smirked and Little Joe smiled.

"When did the ranch buy the Duke?" Tuck asked Hoss.

"Probably a couple weeks ago, and those maps were in it when the title was transferred because I flew her in."

"And I guess you have come here for fuel?"

"Sure, this is where we fuel her."

"And she has been in here before?"

"Sure, a couple times."

Turning to Stephen Tuck said, "Go out and get the number of the fueling crew and verify what this piece of crap just said, please."

"Hold up on that Stephen," said Mark David, "It says here on the Duke site that every serial number is imprinted again underneath the instrument panel on the port side, I'll be right back." Everyone got quiet. It wasn't two minutes Mark was back, "He handed Tuck his phone with a picture of the list of *Original Serial Numbers.*"

"There seems to be some problem here with serial numbers. I am looking at a picture Mark David took of the original serial numbers of all equipment on the Duke and they do not match the ones on the engines or fuselage now, which tells me some one has changed them."

"You get that, boss?" A brief pause ensued. "We will take care of them, no sweat. Of course, no one will find them. See you later." Then, he turned to the others. "Tape Hoss's mouth first."

Mark David walked over and grabbed a handful of hair as he applied the tape. The same was done to Little Joe.

"Okay Dusty, fire away." Tuck nodded at Hoss.

Hoss was hit with a 70,000 volt police Tazer. The big man tried to scream, but only threw mucus out his nose. Using the jacket they had removed from the man, Dusty wiped Hoss's face.

"Now listen, and listen good. I wanted to ask some questions, but the boss said you probably would not cooperate and if you did, you would lie. So since you are just excess baggage, we are supposed to get rid of you."

A questioning look came over Little Joe's face. "You want to say something, Joe?" Buddy said to him.

He nodded.

"Do you have something constructive to say about the plane and kidnapping?" At the word kidnapping, his look changed, but he nodded again.

"I am going to remove this tape and I suggest you say something we want to hear." Buddy yanked the tape off.

"You cannot do this. This is America, and we have rights." The tape went back on.

"That was not constructive, Little Joe," Buddy admonished. "Let me tell you a story." Joe just stared at him. "Now for the story: There once was a sweet lady named Mary Ann. She lived on a mountain, a very happy lady. Then, one day, someone, I am guessing, YOU and someone else maybe named Craig or Drey, something like that, took her down the mountain in a black Hummer pick up. How am I doing? Just stare guys; that is okay. And then Fat Hoss there landed a rented White Duke at an air port. Let's see you have the name here written on the map—Lower Creek, yeah, that is it. Then you flew it south and landed at the Conestoga. Now how am I doing?"

"Before you answer, let me tell you a secret. Mary Ann has a son. He is a law officer, but you probably know that. What you may not know is, he is in this room. Do you read English?" He offered a purposeful pause. "Good, Mary Ann's name is Kirkman. Dusty, show these stupid men who are about to die for a boss they probably hate—how about show him some ID?" Dusty paused for each one to look at the driver's license and his badge. "Now that you know who we are leaving in here with you, we are going to go talk to Andrea, maybe have a coke. Dusty is very upset at someone who has handled his mama. We like to know who is in charge, just who is on the ranch now where Dusty's mama is located, and how are the folks armed. But you do not want to cooperate, so they are yours, Dusty," he said, and then he whispered real low— "Boys, we are not really FBI so we don't know about those rights, lawyers and stuff, and what's more, we do not care. Have a good day."

As everyone started for the door, all of a sudden Hoss started shaking his head wildly. Tuck walked over to him. "Are you trying to tell us something we do not know?" He nodded. "Okay, understand this; if I take this tape off and you tell me another lie or start talking about rights, you see, Hoss, I don't buy that, because Dusty's mama had rights, too. A lie or waste of time and the tape goes back on, and if you yell I will knock all your teeth out, retape your mouth, and let you drown in your own blood, you understand?" Hoss nodded again, his eyes wild. Tuck removed the tape.

Hoss gave a meaningful look to Little Joe. "The jig is up. I ain't frying for nobody."

"You are right there. Now first thing, is Mary

Ann still in the house and is she all right?"

"She is good. We were ordered to treat her with kid gloves, so he musta sold her for megabucks."

"Who else is on the ranch besides Craig and Drey?"

"Andrew, the boss, a Mex cook and a couple girls are usually in the house."

"YOU are doing pretty good so far. Now this is very important—who drives the Hummer?"

A pause, paired with a confused look. "I don't know no Hummer."

"Tape his mouth back shut. He is lying," Tuck said.

"No, no, please, I am not lying!"

Buddy walked over and got in Hoss's face. "This is going to be short and simple, a memory refresher. You landed a plane in North Carolina. A black Hummer pickup was there. Dusty's mama was taken into the Hummer by Little Joe, that guy over there who is about to die." Joe squirmed and furiously shook his head. "Then, Mary Ann was loaded aboard the Duke where you were waiting to fly south. Now think real good, who drives the Hummer?"

Hoss started to cry, in what sounded like relief. "Why you not say it was a black pickup truck? Craig drove it there. I don't know nothing about Hummers; to me it is an ugly big pickup truck."

"Joe," Tuck told the little guy, "remember both your lives depend on this. One strike and you are out. Is Hoss telling the truth?" There was a slight pause, followed by a weak nod.

"You seem to hesitate, Joe. Hold that thought. I will get back to you."

"Okay, how are the men armed and where will they be in the next few hours?"

"The boss will be in the house. He sometimes goes out on his porch to sit after dinner. He carries his pistol in the back. And, his knife, which he prefers, is in the back as well, but up near his neck. All the time on the ranch one of the cowboys wears their guns like Roy Rogers. The other does not have a gun."

"Now just to clarify something in my mind, when Mary Ann is sold, does the buyer come here or do you deliver her?" Tuck asked.

"Every deal is different, but I think this one we are to deliver. I do not know when."

"Is there anything else I need to know?"

"No, that is all I know." Tuck re-taped Hoss's mouth and the man's eyes opened wide in surprise.

"It's all right. If all this is verified, you will be okay." Tuck walked over to Little Joe. "I will not repeat myself. The crime of kidnapping was committed in North Carolina, and they do have a death penalty. So we need to know facts. Cooperation may save your life. I am going to remove the tape. The same rule applies—if you yell I will bash in your teeth and re-tape your mouth and you drown in your blood, understood?" Joe nodded furiously. "One more thing—did Hoss tell me everything?" Joe shook his head, while Hoss looked about to panic. "Seems we have a disagreement." He tore the tape from Little Joe's mouth.

CHAPTER 15

HUMAN VALUE

Accompanied by Missie, Mary Ann headed back to her room to get fresh make up with a touch up of her hair style. A brief back and neck massage and she met the approval of Missie, because it was acknowledged by smile. "Thank you Missie. I know you are trying to make my stay here as comfortable as it can be, and I appreciate it. I have two sweet daughters a little older than you. I know they would do the same for an older woman in trouble."

"Oh, Mistress, you are not in trouble. Andrew says you are headed for riches we can only dream of; we are hoping one day you will remember us, for we would love to work for you. When you get rich enough, you could possibly buy us."

"Oh, sweetie, people are not bought and sold like cattle. People are supposed to be free."

"Oh no, Mistress, we all have value. Andrew says so. He says that me and Mae are worth about fifty thousand dollars. That is a lot of money. We are not sure you would pay that for us."

"Honey I would pay anything for you and Mae. But what do you say, let's cross that bridge when we come to it. Missie, do you have a boyfriend?"

"Oh, I did at one time, but not anymore. Andrew says it is not good for me. So I do not have a boyfriend."

"Well I do, sweetie. Yes, an old lady has a beau. We call him Buck. I miss him so much I could cry." Out of the corner of her eye, she noticed Missie giving her the 'no, no' look, and quickly recovered for the snoopers' benefit. "But I guess that was in a past life. Even that being so, it is still hard for us girls to forget, isn't it?"

"Of course, Mistress, life must be orderly, and to be orderly we must obey orders, so now," she smiled, "it is time for you to have a delicious lunch with Andrew. You are very fortunate, my lady."

"I'm ready, sweetie," Mary Ann said as the thought passed through her mind again: *I must get a plan.*

Again, Andrew stood at the base of the stairs, all

smiles. "My lady, you even look more stunning than usual. I believe the walk outside has done wonders for you."

"To be honest, yes, it was good to get outside and feel free."

"Unfortunately, Mary LaRoach, we know you will never be free as you have thought in the past, but you will enjoy a much better life and on a level that millions upon millions only dream of," he said. "And in leaving that past you will be giving your children something that otherwise they could have only dreamed, thousands of dollars in cash with no obligation."

"If this ever comes to pass, I will honestly be grateful. I don't like to be thought of as being dead, but if that's what it takes…it's okay. But Andrew, I want to keep stressing, that is not my first choice."

"I know that, Mary LaRoach, and your honesty is refreshing. Now let us have some soup and a sandwich."

Thinking, while trying to look interested in the present, was getting easier, *The cook seems to know exactly how I like my food. The Reuben was delicious and the tomato basil soup was the right consistency. Why couldn't I be having lunch with Buck? Lordy, Buck, what you must be thinking. I bet you think I ran off to get away from you. No, you cannot think that. I know you wouldn't. Is anyone looking for me yet? Oh yes, they must be looking. I missed Samantha's birthday party. They know I am either dead or locked up somewhere. I have never missed a birthday party for my grandkids. Problem is, they are looking around Lenoir and here I am in Calajap, Egypt or somewhere. Those palm trees outside are sure not in Caldwell county.* She looked across at Andrew and smiled. "The food around here is delicious. You must have a real chef."

"Cook does his job. He sometimes improvises, but mostly the food is edible. Soon, you will be fed by a world famous chef. And you will forget about this food. Now, on another note, my dear, I am sure the girls have mentioned they would like to follow you to riches. I have no problem with that, if the man will pay, let's say, sixty thousand American dollars, plus expenses, I will deliver them unharmed and in good health."

"Your lack of humanity never ceases to amaze me. How can you do these things?"

"Ah, Mary LaRoach, snide and snarky just do not fit you, my dear, but again I do understand. I have explained, humans are a very good trading commodity and they have been since time began. They are tough and do not spoil in transit. You are a great example of that—you look delicious. Your looks do not picture your age, my dear."

"Every lady loves a compliment, especially if it pertains to not looking her age," Mary Ann admitted.

He clapped his hands and the girls appeared. "I have enjoyed our lunch, but I must return to my office and get some work done. Now off with you, girls."

"Missie will accompany you to the porch and I will get you a good cup of coffee."

"Could you ladies have coffee with me?" Mary Ann asked.

"Only if you insist. We would never impose."

"Then I insist, my sweeties. Let's have coffee and talk about boys." They all laughed.

They spent a couple hours on the patio, talking

about nothing. They all were painfully aware of the spy tech equipment around. At one point, they heard the airplane take off. *Now where is that plane going?*

"I wonder where that plane is going?" Mary Ann mused, aloud, this time.

"I think it is better that we do not wonder, Mistress. We should enjoy this sun and relax," Mae said firmly.

Then suddenly, through the patio doors, they heard Andrew shout, "Everyone inside, now!" The conciliatory tone was gone; the girls jumped immediately and Mary Ann knew something bad had happened. Fear showed in the girls' faces.

"My dear Mary Ann, I just received word that your benefactor has just been killed. The foolish old man exposed himself unnecessarily and was hit by several bullets. Not a terrible thing, since I collected three quarters of your price up front, but it does present a dilemma. When I am procuring young sex toys for these men, the man's death is not a problem. There is an open market for the young sex objects and all I have to do is call the next man on the list."

"So what you are saying is that this old woman is excess baggage now. Who else would need an old woman?!" Mary Ann said a little stronger than she meant to.

"I will excuse your brashness this time, Mary Ann, but take note—at this point I have no incentive to keep you alive. You will speak to me with permission only. Now to brass tacks, as you Southerners like to say. You have become disposable; you should not take this personally, as I have been honest with you. This is business." Seeing Mary Ann wanted to say something, he added, "Yes, Mary Ann?"

At least I have my name back. "Do I have any choice?"

"There is always a choice. Yours is life or death—that simple."

"Is it that simple?"

"Yes, my dear. Cook can use some help in the kitchen. Missie and Mae need a mother's touch. Oh yes, there is a slot you can fit in, but it requires complete loyalty, I mean complete. Now to be crude, as you would say, but to let you know exactly what I mean, Mae, tell Mary Ann what will happen to you if you are not loyal to me?"

"If I am not loyal to Mr. Andrew, he will turn me over to the men to enjoy themselves with and then he will kill me." As she finished, her eyes were gleaming, on the verge of tears.

"And my dear Mae, how do you know this?"

"Because I have seen it happen, Mr. Andrew, and I believe it." Now tears were flowing down her cheeks and Mary Ann was getting sick to her stomach. She started to speak, but the look on Andrew's face said, 'No.'

"Do we understand each other, Mary Ann?"

Mary Ann only nodded. *Now I know how the girls have been feeling the whole time. I am going to live under that threat as well, but I have lived many years and these girls have not. They need time to live and love.*

"There is another bed in the girls' room. You will sleep there. They will explain the schedule. Now that you are hired help, as soon as you are situated, report to the cook. Missie you will stay with her at all times and work with Cook also. Now Missie, you will tell me if Mary Ann says or does anything that appears stupid, want you?"

"Yes sir, Mr. Andrew, you know I am loyal, and believe in order."

The son of a dog sure knows how to put pressure on. I need a plan, now more than ever...

The room was located in the basement. It had two windows for light—well, more slits than windows, about four inches high and two feet wide. There would be no leaving this room except by the door. To one side stood a bathroom, several chairs, and two sets of bunk beds. "Mistress, you take the lower bunk here," Missie said. "We will get you some clothes soon."

"Please Missie, I wish you and Mae would call me Mary Ann. We are evidently in this boat together. And besides, Mistress makes me sound old." They both laughed together.

They reported to the cook and Mary Ann was assigned to wash the huge stack of pots, pans, and cutlery. It actually felt good to be doing something. This was one thing she could do and enabled her to think as she worked. *I never in my life thought anyone could talk about killing a person in as casual a manner as swatting a fly. This is one serious thing you are locked into now, Mary Ann. Can I make it until someone figures out where I am?* Thinking of that sort of depressed her because in reality, how could anyone know where she was? *So what? I have been on my own many times. This may be tougher, but with God's help, I am going to get out of here. But to tell you the truth, the faith gets a little low when someone tells you, "If you give me any trouble, I will kill you."*

"Mary Ann, I need the big flat pan as soon as you can get to it," Cook said.

The cook had been nice to her but distant. It was easy to see he was in the same situation as the girls, and now her. She quickly got him the pan and he thanked her with a smile and a softer tone, which made Mary Ann feel better.

Sherry had called just before she was dragged out of her house. In confidence, Sherry had told her some stuff about her new husband—cloak and dagger things. *Now if she and Jerry were to get concerned, maybe with Dusty's help they might be able to find me. I did try to leave one hint by saying something about my Calebie or Cabie and how sweet he was all the time. I know she will think that was strange or stupid, but she will know it is something out of left field.*

She was still deep in thought when a man came through the kitchen door wearing a gun on his hip. "Hello Craig, have you guys been moving any cows?" Craig asked.

"Yeah, there are a couple renegades in this herd. Mr. Andrew said to look for a young heifer to slaughter. Me'n Drey gonna drive her down to the barn and do it. We might party tonight. Too bad you cannot come. Maybe we will slip you a drink, if you will cook us a big steak."

"Now you know I am not allowed to drink, Craig, although sometimes I would sure like one, but I ain't that stupid. I will have you guy's supper ready in about five minutes. There is some orange juice in the reefer if you want."

"I heard the plane leave; you want me to wrap two meals in tin foil to keep it warm?"

"Might be a good idea. Sometimes they try to look up a woman or two in Arcadia." The cook winced at the words. "Uh, I mean Atlanta or somewhere; can't tell about them crazy boys you know in Atlanta or Alaska."

The last part of the conversation seemed rather tense, and she had heard the name of a town in Florida. *Arcadia is near, thank God. At least know I am still in the USA and not Mexico or an island.*

Cook soon had the dinners packed and Craig left through the same door he had entered. In less than a minute, there was a conversation coming through, but she could not make out what was said.

****

Outside, Andrew had approached after the food was loaded on the golf cart. "Craig, we need to talk."

"Yes sir, Mr. Andrew."

"What are the rules about speaking to the help in the house and the using a name of any location?"

"I know I ain't supposed to pass the time of day, but we just decided to wrap the other boys' dinner up so it would not get c-cold," Craig said, sorta stuttering.

"You are right handed, I know. Let me see your left hand." When he raised his hand, Andrew did the same, his finger on the trigger of a pistol. He fired and took the small finger off clean.

"My God, you shot my finger off! Why did you do that?"

Andrew handed him a towel. "You said one word you should not have said. Do you understand?"

"It was a mistake, Mr. Andrew, but my God, that was my finger. It hurts like Hell."

"I imagine it does; now get on back to the barn and have Drey wrap it up. He is our animal doctor and you fit the bill of a dumb animal tonight. Now just a word of advice—that shot could have been through your stupid head, and the next time it will be, is that understood?" Craig nodded. "Now get to the barn before you bleed to death."

Inside, they heard the gun shot, and the yell. Mary Ann looked around to see that Cook and Missie were busy working like nothing had happened. *Dear Lord, what kind of place is this?* Then she began to pray for deliverance ... very seriously.

CHAPTER 16

THE FBI IS CALLED OFF

Up in Lenoir, they too were looking at the photos of the Conestoga. They had listened to the conversations and recorded them. Matt and Luke, along with the FBI agents, were looking for a possible assault plan. They needed to know in what part of the house Andrew's sleeping quarters were located most of all, but it would have been good to know where everyone slept.

Was there a time the plane was due back at the ranch? They all knew that, since the notorious Hoss and Little Joe were in custody, the assault on the ranch should happen soon. The crew in Lenoir wanted to be down there for the action and finale. However, the task would fall to the ones who had made the trip mainly for reconnaissance. This was proving that Jerry knew how to plan, and to take many possibilities into account. Jerry had been burned a couple times by assuming the wrong parameters. Over the years he had learned to plan, just in case the unexpected slapped them in the face.

Then a phone rang on the belt of Agent Mix. She took the call and, after a few 'Yes, sirs', she hung up.

"Jerry, we are out of here. I told the boss that this was absolutely a kidnapping and the boss says, if you want, you are officially deputized to act as the FBI. However, a higher priority has been dealt. The security level has been raised by Homeland Security due to a terrorist breach on the Southern border. All agents not occupied on a HOT project are recalled, and we fly out of Morganton in forty minutes. One J.K. LaRoach, a guy we have been trying to find for a long time, has been killed already. Good luck, I mean that and also wish we could stay. I sincerely mean that, too. We wish you the best."

"Good luck to you two also. Thanks, you have been a great help, and we will not forget it."

Sherry gave them both a big hug as they left, and thanked them again.

Jerry grouped with Matt and Luke. "What do you

have so far?"

"It looks like the best approach is a vertical attack. The land near the house is flat except for one rise. There are several hammocks of live oaks that would give some cover, but time is against us for a trip overland to get there," recounted Matt.

"We gave some thought to Stella flying the Duke into the ranch and taxiing up to the house. Possibly here." Luke pointed to a small covered area that appeared to be a small building of sorts. "That could be a storage building or a well house, but it is some cover."

"Since we do not know the fire power inside the house, a direct attack could be disastrous," Jerry commented. "Let me get them back on the line to see if they have anything else of import from the two down there."

CHAPTER 17

POSSIBLE EXTRA TROUBLE FOR MARY ANN

The call came in from Jerry. Both ends were

using the phone speakers to include as many of the team as possible. That way, everyone would be on the same page.

The tape had been removed from Little Joe's mouth, and he began to talk. "Hoss does not know it all; he is seldom at the house. The lady is doing well and walks outside at times with the girls always with her. She is now called Mary LaRoach. Mr. Andrew has sold this lady for a huge sum of money, maybe millions of American dollars."

"And you know this how?" Tuck asked.

(In Lenoir, Jerry quickly nodded to Josh, indicating to start a search for LaRoach.)

"I overheard a phone conversation once before we flew north," Little Joe said.

"Does Andrew sell people on a regular basis?" Buddy asked.

"*Si*, yes, we are told to pick up people two or three times a month. Most are beautiful Latino ladies from the street. It is easy with them; they are impressed by the big Hummer because they see money and we dress cool. We use needles supplied by Andrew and they are soon asleep for an hour or so. There are times when we fly them directly to the buyer. The cook and the two girls we picked up as well, but they were refused by a buyer, so they are here at the ranchero."

Buddy asked Hoss if Little Joe was telling the truth and he nodded. "Now Joe, when is the plane due back at the ranch?"

"We have no set time; sometimes we can find a willing lady here and have some beer and tequila before we return. We are not slaves, and we are free."

"If you go in after dark, do you have lights?"

"No, Hoss is a good pilot. The cowboys know to have a light for him to aim at when they hear the plane approach and we always get in good."

After more questions, they learned that Andrew slept on the first floor near the south wall. The girls and the cook had rooms in the basement. All visitors slept on the second floor. "Okay, you guys are doing quite well; I even believe some of this stuff. So, where is the Hummer right now?" Buddy took the tape back off Hoss.

"It is in the barn, or it was when we flew out,"

Hoss said in a deflated tone.

"Will the cowboys leave the ranch while you are gone?"

"No way, Andrew would kill them."

"Speaking of killing," Buddy said, "how many people have you buried on the ranch, and where?"

The two guys looked at each other in defeat. "You tell them, Joe."

"We killed no one, believe me, but we have buried two ladies and three men."

"Who killed them?"

"He will kill us man. He thinks no more of shooting a man or woman than slapping a fly. Do you promise to protect us?"

"Oh yes, when the real FBI gets here, they will honor any agreements we make. They are just waiting for us to solve this for them. They will probably pay you with your life, to hang your Mr. Andrew. So you are saying that Andrew has killed five people that you know of." Both men nodded. "And where did you bury them?"

"They are under the patio out back of the house. After each one was buried, we had to mix cement and cover them. Joe is good with concrete finishing. If we had not agreed to bury them, he would have killed us. We had no choice," Hoss cried, while Little Joe nodded in agreement.

Tuck flipped off the speaker and spoke to Jerry, "Did you get all that, boss?"

"Yeah, we got it recorded. Tuck, are you on the speaker down there?"

"No, not now. What's up?"

"You will understand without me doing a lot of detail, but most likely Mary Ann is in deeper trouble, or will be, so I do not want Dusty to go off half cocked. If Mary Ann was scheduled to be sold to an old man named LaRoach, the FBI just shot him dead down at the Mexican border, so the deal will be off. He was a big kingpin in the drug and terror business. Josh is still digging on that. I am going to put Matt and Luke on a conference call with you guys to let you know what they are looking at for an approach to the Ranch. By the way, our two agents were just called to the TexMex border where the trouble is. And you guys with the FBI badges *are* FBI if you need to be, by order of the station agent in Raleigh."

Jerry listened as the two groups talked. He was put at ease because of the similarities in the ideas. The final option chosen was an evening attack. With Stella telling them what she could do with the Duke, they had decided on two jumpers to land on the widow's walk on top of the house. The jumpers would be coming down pretty much vertically by tight circles; tentatively, Buddy and Stephen were the jumpers. After a little discussion, Stephen gave way to Mark David who had just re-qualified for his wings. So the jumpers would be Buddy first, followed by Mark David. Stella was positive she could cut her engines out of hearing range and glide the light Duke down to one thousand feet for a fast jump. Then, she'd glide past the house before restarting the engines. Her plan was to do a tight 360 degree turn and land ending at the barn.

The idea was to leave the landing lights on to take away the cowboys' night vision when she cut them. Before the plane came to a halt, the door would be open, ready for Tuck, Dusty and Stephen to jump out. Dusty was going to take the cowboy outside while the other two took the one inside.

They were counting on the description by Hoss and Little Joe to be accurate. They had drawn it out and went through it several times.

Then, the tricky part of the plan was to use the Hummer to get back to the house before any alarm was sounded. Stella insisted on driving the truck to allow the troops to concentrate on getting into the house. They were still trying to figure out whether to go with Stella's idea of her driving up the steps and through the front door, discharging the troops, and backing out. Tuck suggested ripping the doors off to make easy exits. Everyone agreed with that idea. Josh was tasked with finding the fastest way to remove the doors.

Leaving the guys to mull over the plan looking for holes, Tuck and Buddy went out to talk to Andrea. "Hey, my friend, is it about time to close up shop? Do you need to get home?"

"Yes, it is time, but I cannot close as long as you guys are here. But nah, I don't need to go home, although they will not pay over time here."

"Okay, we are authorized to pay you triple time if you will hang with us. Why don't you call the sheriff? We need to talk to him." Buddy took out two one hundred dollar bills and handed them to Andrea. "This is too much, my friend." Buddy just smiled.

Andrea got the sheriff on the phone, told him the FBI wanted to talk to him, and handed the phone to Tuck. "Yes, Sheriff, we are at the airport and have a couple of kidnappers for you. There are some extenuating circumstances, and there are at least three others on the loose, but we know where they are. If you can spare a couple of cars and at least four men, I don't think you will regret it."

"I think we can handle that. See you in ten minutes."

By the time the local sheriff arrived, the plan was set and they had the gate codes for him to use to get into the ranch. A time was established. When the sheriff heard the airplane engines restart, they would head up the mile driveway, driving slowly until they saw the Hummer heading for the house.

Buddy took him aside. "Sheriff, we do not want to be here; therefore, on all records, we prefer to be invisible. However there is a sweet lady in that house that we want to take back to North Carolina to her family. The two men that you know as Hoss and Little Joe Kidnapped this senior lady who is seventy years old. She does not need to go through a trial as a witness. The humanitarian thing is to forget her and that is what we want. We are going to leave the confessions of the two kidnappers that we have in custody with you. They have been very cooperative. I am not sure about the three victims in the ranch house right now, but the two men in there are eye witnesses to five murders and that is on tape. They have told where the bodies are buried. After the bust is made and all is secure, we are out of it. We want to fly out of here taking the lady back to her family and a plane that was stolen from Sarasota last week back to its owner in Sarasota. The owner is a senior citizen also and depends on this aircraft for his living. If it were tied up as evidence for months, it would severely hurt his income and business."

"You can have the bust with our blessings. If it goes wrong you have every right to go public and we will take the blame; we have enough to deal with on a federal level. you can record this agreement; I have no problem with that. We just want out of here. The son of the lady who was kidnapped is here and on our team. He is a County Mountie from Gaston County, North Carolina. Can you live with that?"

"Of course I can, if it is as you describe it, and of course this is already being recorded."

Smiling, Tuck said, "I figured as much. I would offer you more proof but you will be hard pressed to find an agent who will have time to talk now. Homeland Security and the FBI have a big problem on the TexMex border that is taking every available agent."

The sheriff took the gate codes along with the instructions and gave an estimated time to be at the gate; then they went in to see his prisoners. He looked at the two trussed up suspects and smiled. "You are kidding me. Hoss and Little Joe kidnapped a woman? Guys, did y'all do that?"

Both men nodded sheepishly. The sheriff continued, "I have met Andrew. He came in a few years back when he bought the Conestoga and introduced himself as the CEO of a 'Not-for-Profit organization. He would be raising some cattle and doing business in town. He seemed nice enough but you could tell he thought a lot of himself. And you boys actually saw the man kill someone?"

Both men nodded again, this time with their eyes down cast.

"But they have been very cooperative, Sheriff. I think any break they can get would be good," Buddy said. "I have a feeling at the ranch, you are gonna find enough evidence that will solve hundreds of open cases."

"Deputy Thomas here will drop them off at the jail … Deputy, inform the jailer they are not to have use of a phone until I call or return."

"Hey Buddy," came Jerry's voice over the speaker phone. It startled the sheriff and his deputy a little. "Let me introduce myself. Sheriff, I am Dr. Jerry Wiley, CEO of Wiley Industries. The lady who was kidnapped is very close to me; that is why I am interested. The men you see there and I are at present official FBI agents, by order of Agent in Charge Beatty of the North Carolina office of the FBI. Please don't take offense but I need to ask you an open question that I would prefer to ask in private, yet that is not feasible—Do you feel confident in your ability to personally arrest this Andrew guy at the ranch? I ask because the troops already have a good plan, except for one part: a controlled confrontation."

"Dr. Wiley, I take no offense. I can confidently say that I will enforce the solemn oath I took as sheriff. If required, I would arrest the President of the United States. Does that answer your question?"

"I will let my man Buddy down there answer for me. Is that good enough, Buddy?"

"Yeah Boss, we all agree this seems to be one standup guy. Now what is this about a change of plans?"

"Well, I don't like the idea of my pilot driving a Hummer up to that house, not knowing the real defense or offense from inside. We have seen that backfire. You guys work it out, but I would prefer the sheriff knock on the door with a good story of how he got past the gate and about Hoss and Joe being in trouble downtown. He'll say he is there out of respect and has come to notify him personally, etc. etc. And then at the proper time, the sheriff informs him he is under arrest. Of course, this Andrew will be on guard, but there is less chance of encountering a surprise you cannot handle. Talk it over and look at it from that angle. That way it will be officially an arrest by the sheriff, without any federal intervention."

"The sheriff agrees so it's affirmative, Jerry. We will work on it and let you know. I guess we can sign off now. Keep looking into the LaRoach character for us; we are very curious about him. Hug Sherry for us and assure her we are gonna bring Mary Ann back!"

Outside, Stella and Mark David had been checking out the Duke and were happy with the results. It was fully fueled now. She learned that Mark David could fly this bird. They took it out on the runway and gave it a few runs before bringing it back to the fueling spot. Therefore, if all went well at the ranch, after a shuttle or two, Stella would take her plane and Mark David could deliver the Duke back to its owner. After finishing with their task, they walked back inside to learn of the change in plans being discussed. The new plan seemed to make more sense.

"Crap," voiced Stella, "I wanted to drive that Hummer through the front door. Jerry is a killjoy." That gave everyone a good laugh and broke some tension. Sometimes that is all it takes.

The equipment had been loaded aboard the

Duke and it was ready to go. The team was only waiting for more darkness. Everyone was doing their own thing to get mentally ready for the fast ten minutes they hoped it would take. Part of the team stayed with the Sheriff and joined him on the way to the ranch.

CHAPTER 18

NEW HOME IN THE BASEMENT

The kitchen prepared a great meal for Andrew and as usual, Missie served. Evidently, Andrew did not get terribly upset at a business deal going sour; he seemed to take it in stride. Mary Ann was observing now from the inside. There was very little chit chat in the kitchen. It appeared the only conversations concerned the job at hand. Mary Ann assumed that most of the silence was because of her presence. A sense of mistrust filled the air because one person could get another killed here in this crazy house. The others had survived by not making waves and following the rules, and when in doubt they would err on the safe side.

"Mary Ann, if you would please mop the floor after Missie sweeps, we will close the kitchen. I will see you two in the morning at six thirty. No guests are planned so it will be a simple day. I can tell that you have spent a lot of time in a kitchen. That will be good. If Mr. Andrew will allow it, I am sure you can add some variety to our cuisine. I am glad to have met you. Please follow the rules; life is much easier when everyone follows the guidelines set forth by Mr. Andrew."

"I am glad to meet you also, I have wanted to tell you that the meals I have eaten here, which you prepared, have been delicious and in some cases, the best I've ever eaten. Now that I may be working here, I need to know how you want to be addressed."

"My dear, my name matters no more; simply call me Cook. It has become my name and my occupation," he said, smiling. "Life is good. I enjoy cooking and good food, so working here allows me to pursue my passion. I hope you can adjust. We might make a good team."

"Thanks for the vote of confidence, Cook. I have

always been a fast learner and I will adjust."

After mopping the floor, she looked up at the clock. It was nearing seven o'clock when they left the kitchen. She and Missie went straight down to their room. Mae was already in bed and reading a book when they entered.

The girls started chatting away. Mae had seen a beautiful red bird as she was redoing the bedroom Mary Ann had occupied. She sort of frowned as she said to Mary Ann, "Missie said you wanted us to address you as Mary Ann. It will take some getting used to. I am sure this must be a big let down from the opulence of that bedroom to this."

"Sweetie, you have no idea how much better this is to me. I love sharing a room with you two, but I feel like I am imposing," Mary Ann remarked with a laugh.

"Never, you are one of the nicest people we have met. And your smile is contagious. I worry that you may forget some of the rules, because you are one tough lady. Neither of us wants to see you hurt. I will say no more on that subject, okay?"

"Girls, as I told Cook tonight, I am a fast learner.

I do not want to be hurt and most of all, I do not want you or Cook hurt. So if you will allow me to be your 'good' stepmother, I would love it and be honored."

They enjoyed some busy talk. Mary Ann and Missie took turns in the shower, and soon, they were all ready to go to bed. Just then at about eight thirty, Mary Ann heard a loud click. With a questioning look, she turned to Mae who was closest, "What was that?"

"Mama, that is our security. Now no one can get in to bother us. The door will be opened in the morning at six o'clock."

Mary Ann made a funny face with her bottom lip, winked, nodded, and lay down in the semi-darkness to get some rest. She felt tired, but it was sort of a good tired. She needed the work to occupy her mind. Furthermore, she had a lot to pray about, and much thinking to do. *Well girl, you went from riches to rags mighty quick. What was that quote from long ago? 'Oh how the mighty have fallen'—not that I had been mighty, but I have fallen in value, according to Andrew. I would like to tell that man, I feel better locked in this basement than upstairs wondering what rich hell I was headed for. Now Lord, this is me again, Mary Ann. I used to sing a song, Lord, Not my father, not my mother, not my sister, but it's me, oh Lord, standing in the need of prayer. I've asked you for a lot of silly stuff in my life but this is different. You know that well, don't you? I want you to comfort my kids. Yes, I know they aren't kids any more, but you know what I mean. There is something I like about talking to you, Lord, you listen. That makes me feel good.*

I would like for my son to open that door right now, walk in and hug his mama tight. But if that doesn't happen, I can wait until your time. I probably ain't gonna like it here and I might complain, but I really don't mean it. I trust you. Shucks, you have never failed me. Now these girls, I believe they are good girls. The Cook seems to be a nice man. So when you deliver me from this place, could you take them also? The prayer continued on until Mary Ann fell asleep.

****

Prayers heal souls. Next door to the girls' bedroom in the basement, Cook, who had been raised by a loving Catholic mother, knelt down and prayed, as he had every night for a couple of years. He prayed to rejoin his wife. He prayed for a happy family. He wanted to see smiling faces around a

Christmas tree.

****

The basement rooms were semi-dark, never fully dark. Upstairs in his office, Andrew could see the Cook as he knelt. Speaking to the empty room and the black and white screen, he smirked. "Cook, you are a fool, but your rituals keep you in line. You kneel there every night knowing I am seeing you. I would bet a thousand dollars that Mary Ann is praying to her God as she lies there. Karl Marx was exactly right because I have two examples here to prove that religion is the opium of the masses. Stupid religious people will never learn. Believing some invisible god is standing listening, they being too stupid to realize billions of silly folk like them are praying all over the world in many languages and religions. So yes Cook, keep praying you and Mary Ann will make a good team." He shook his head as he finished his evening wine.

To Andrew, the setback with Mary Ann's sale was water under the bridge. One thing he had learned was, looking back is unworthy unless you learn something. He smiled thinking of the orders he'd received just that day. Five orders for sex objects and two orders for men. He was amazed at the increase in calls for young boys and men since the president himself had basically stated that homosexuality was okay. "As long as the pay is good I couldn't care less about the right or wrong of it." He smiled to himself as again he realized he was talking out loud to an empty room. *Maybe I need some company, but who can a man trust?*

CHAPTER 19

THE NEW PLAN OF ATTACK

Gathered around a small table, everyone concerned with the night visit to the Ranch Conestoga was looking at the rough drawing that had been used earlier. They had already made the prisoners more comfortable. All the duck tape had been removed but their hands and feet were held by the nylon lock bands.

"Sheriff, our original plan was for our pilot flying

the ranch plane to drop two men over the ranch house in the early evening. The pilot was going to drop them on a glide, then restart the engines and land. The jumpers were going to do tight circles down to the roof. We were going to depend on the landing lights to take the night vision from one cowboy, leaving him vulnerable for an easy takedown. That was using the information that Hoss had given us. He said one cowboy always comes out with a light anytime they arrived after dark. At the same time the plane guide was being neutralized, another man would leave the plane and go into the barn and secure the remaining cowboy. Any necessary gunfire would have been with silenced weapons to keep the element of surprise at the house. That was roughly the original plan. Now that has changed. After further thinking we were paying attention to the secondary threat first. If something had gone wrong, and a wrong move had notified the ranch house, we would have additional trouble we did not need. Now I think using the updated info from the boss and with your presence and cooperation, the new approach will work much better. Not a walk in the park, but it looks better." Buddy nodded to Tuck.

"This is sorta off the cuff, but now, with your help, Sheriff, I think we can ignore the cowboys initially. Let me go through this, and then we will see if we can knock holes in it. For safety's sake, we still need someone in that house when you knock on the door. So instead of the silent treatment of the plane, the jumpers will jump from a higher altitude and not worry about tight circles and engine noise, since we are going in at night. They will give us early warning by a flash light signal a few hundred feet above the house to let us know they are near. We should be able to see them regardless. They will be using black night chutes, of course. Once they have access to the house, they will key the radio transmitter twice. As soon as they are in the house, they will not go downstairs until they hear the doorbell and know you—we—are at the door. Okay, any of you ... problems?"

"How many jumpers?" the sheriff asked.

"We have two and both qualified and trained in night jumps."

"What happens if one jumper misses the house?" Stella asked.

"If a jumper misses the house, we will get two

three-click responses on the radio. If both miss the roof, we will get a very quiet radio call. We will only key a one click answer to acknowledge. If that scenario occurs they will enter on the ground level when the front door is opened. We are hoping at that time the alarms will be turned off."

"What about the cowboys you talked about?" the sheriff asked.

"Once the house is secure, we will drive or walk down to the hangar. We will then signal Stella to land the plane. It will be much simpler to have men outside than on the plane. What do you think?"

"I'd like my deputies to take care of the cowboys, if all goes well in the house," the sheriff spoke.

"I certainly have no problem with that. Sounds like a plan," Buddy said.

"One other thing, our plan calls for a confrontation at the front door. Hoss tells us that Andrew keeps a gun in the small of his back and a knife at his back up at the neck, you know, for throwing. He says the man is good with gun and knife, and he once saw him hit a scurrying rat."

"Thanks for the heads up. If we are going to do

this at ten, we had better get going. The ranch is about thirty minutes by road. Who goes with me?"

"That will be me, Stephen and Deputy Dusty," Tuck said. "Let's get suited up. I recommend body armor for everyone."

"I agree with that. Let me send my new friends Hoss and Little Joe down to the jailer first. It won't take but a few minutes."

About nine fifteen, the cars headed for the Conestoga. Buddy said goodbye to Andrea and okayed their plans for using the landing field a couple times later that evening or early morning. Then the rest of the crew headed for the plane. Both jumpers checked the chutes underneath the lights and got suited up. As usual, they checked each other to ensure radio, flashlight, silenced handgun, Tazer, hand grenade, and flash-bang were securely attached. The customary tap on the helmet and they climbed aboard and Stella headed the Duke skyward.

En-route on the ground, the sheriff recited the phony story he planned to use, about the boys roughing up one of the Arcadia bar ladies, and he had to keep them overnight, etc. Tuck nodded, agreeing that the sheriff had a good line. *That kind of imagination helps in most lines of work.*

At the gate, Tuck asked the sheriff to hold on while Stephen checked the electronics for a silent alarm that might announce the gate being opened. Stephen was out about five minutes. When he returned, he said, "Good thinking Tuck, there was a transmitter. I disabled it and we are good."

Both cars keyed the code into the gate keypad and they were inside of the ranch boundaries. The cars eased on up the road a bit, their lights off, awaiting some lights from the sky and clicks on the radio. Very faintly, they heard the twin engines of the Duke. "How long before we see a light?" the sheriff asked.

"They are at about ten thousand feet up, so they will freefall probably about forty-five seconds. The free fall is at 120 miles per hour; they will fall a thousand feet every five and a half seconds. So it won't be long."

****

Up in the plane, Stella was holding steady at ten thousand feet. By her calculations, she gave a

"GO!" She counted five seconds and yelled, "GO!" again. Both of her passengers were now airborne. "God be with you, guys," she said aloud as she started her lazy circle, praying all the time that the plan would work perfectly.

"I just saw a chute open," the sheriff said, "and there is the other one."

"The event is past the point of no return. Let's take a deep breath and start rolling slowly." Tuck felt the car rock a little. "Crap, was that the wind?"

"Yep, that was a big gust. Not good for the jumpers, is it?"

"Nope, but they are both good. They will handle it."

Within thirty seconds, they got a three-click signal, then after five seconds, they got another three-click signal. "At least one is on the widow's walk and will be in the house. Very seldom is there an alarm on the second floor. Either man can open the doors in the dark with no problem."

"Will the ground guy break the door in after I ring the bell?"

"Negative. He will unlock the door, but not open it until he is sure the alarm is off. He might even see Andrew disarm the alarm system; that would be a plus. Now, according to our diagram from Hoss and Joe, he will be able to see the front door clearly from his vantage point. So I am sure one or both of our guys will have a weapon trained on Andrew within seconds of seeing him open the door."

"They are that good?"

"Oh yeah, they are that good. Okay, it has been five minutes; let's get this show on the road. As we figured, he will probably turn on lights and view who is outside over a video monitor, and we want him to see only uniforms, Showtime." The cars pulled up in front of the house.

Climbing the steps, the sheriff rang the bell. The lights came on.

"It is very late to be ringing a bell after bypassing security on my gate and trespassing," it was Andrew's voice over the speakers.

Crap, Tuck thought, *very stupid not to think about a speaker.*

"Mr. Andrew, this is Sheriff Wise of Desoto

County. I need to speak with you. Your boys gave me the code to get through the gate. I am on official business so it is not trespassing. I really hated to come but the guys said you would kill them if I didn't explain." The sheriff was doing well winging it with his bit of humor. He continued without a break, "I told them I didn't think it was that drastic, but they insisted."

That is a pretty good tap dance, Sheriff.

"I see a lot of uniforms to deliver a message, sir."

"I have three new deputies who needed some training; I thought the ride would do them good. Is there a problem with that, Mr. Andrew? If it makes you feel more comfortable, I will send them back to the car. I really do not want any trouble for a simple face to face message."

"Please, I am from a country where uniforms mean trouble. You will excuse my fears. Yes, dispatch some, if you please."

"No problem sir, I think I do understand." The sheriff motioned for three of his deputies to head back out to the cars, the cars sat parked in the dark, so they did not enter their vehicle, but stood on alert.

Mark David listened at the portico door as he gave each hinge a shot of lubricant for insurance. He was also seeing Andrew as he viewed the screen. He assumed by now Buddy had arrived at the top of the stairs. Every muscle in his body drew tight. He watched as Andrew casually checked his handgun and returned it to his flat holster in his back. The man also checked the knife, while talking easily and confidently to the sheriff. He was searching the screen for something he might have missed. Evidently satisfied, he pressed some buttons on the security panel and then moved calmly to the door. Mark David immediately eased the door open and stepped inside his silenced pistol aimed at Andrew's center of mass. *You are one cool dude Andy boy, but be good or you'll be dead.*

Andrew opened the door about half way. "Now what is this all about, Sheriff?"

"Hi, Mr. Andrew, I am very sorry to bother you. Hoss and Little Joe flew into town this afternoon and visited a couple bars downtown. They wanted to play with one of the local girls and she didn't want to oblige. I am sorry to say they banged her up pretty badly; she is in the hospital, so I had to arrest them." As the sheriff spoke, Andrew withdrew a few inches inside the house.

"Please step outside, Mr. Andrews. It is hard to talk like this."

Mark tensed; the pistol was coming out. In a flash, the sheriff was looking down the barrel of Andrew's gun. A third eye appeared on Andrew's forehead and at the same time, he saw fire come from the pistol in Andrew's hand, and at close range he felt like he had just been kicked by a mule. Mark and Buddy had fired from their positions at the same instant Tuck had fired from the shadows out front. Andrew's body was spun around by the impacts, but not fast enough to save the sheriff. It was all over in less than five seconds. Tuck was on Andrew immediately to make sure he was out of the picture at the same time Buddy was checking the sheriff, laying him back and making him comfortable before turning him over to Tuck.

All the deputies had drawn their weapons and took up defensive positions around their sheriff. By then, Buddy, Mark David, and Dusty were securing the house. After they were satisfied that all was secure on the first and second floors, the three descended to the basement. To their surprise, everything was dimly lit and easy to maneuver.

Quietly, they checked the open rooms and found no one. Two rooms were obviously barred. Going to the nearest door, Buddy lifted the bar and set it aside. Dusty slowly opened the door, and Mark David stepped inside. He could see a man on the bed, eyes wide open. "Did God send you?" he asked.

"I hope so," Buddy said. "Who are you?"

"I am the cook. Does Mr. Andrew know that you are here?"

"Probably not. He is dead. Are you a prisoner?"

"If Mr. Andrew is dead and God sent you, I am not."

"Cook, we are with the sheriff's department. We were here to arrest Mr. Andrew but he would not cooperate."

"Are the girls next door safe?" Cook asked anxiously. Mark David gave a 'stay here' hand signal.

With that, the three left the cook's room. They used the same procedure, except this time, Dusty entered first. His eyes immediately went to his mother who appeared to be waking up. "Mama?" he said, his voice breaking. "Mama?"

"Dusty!" Mary Ann screamed. "This dream seems so real, is that really you?"

Dusty ran and grabbed his mother and squeezed her. "Yes Mama, it is me. You are safe."

The three men watched as the cook ran by them and grabbed one of the girls. Guns were drawn and pointed his direction. "Back off, Cook," Buddy ordered.

The cook turned, tears streaming down his face. "This is my wife and I have not been allowed to touch her for two years."

"Then get that woman and give her a hug and a kiss for you and all of us." Buddy laughed.

"Oh Missie, how wonderful! I would never have guessed that Cook was your husband," Mary Ann said. "This is wonderful."

Mae seemed to be in shock. When Missie could

break away, she went to Mae and sat beside her on the bed. "Tell them honey, tell them."

"Are the Cowboys okay?" she asked Buddy.

"We haven't checked yet. We have a plane landing shortly and then we plan to take care of the cowboys. What is the problem?"

"The cowboy Drey is my husband. He was taken months before I was. He has played the game as we did, because he had no choice. Please do not hurt him. The other son of a dog, Craig, is Drey's handler. Kill him!"

"Only if we have to, lady. We came for justice only, not revenge."

"Death would be justice. He and Andrew are killers."

"Let's go upstairs and sort this out," Mark David said as he pointed to the door.

Upstairs, they found the sheriff, who lay across the table, still moving. Tuck and a deputy stood beside him. Looking over at the guys as they came up from the basement, Tuck informed them, "The Sheriff will be okay. His body armor saved him, but you know it is like being kicked by a horse."

At that time, the deputy was helping his sheriff up. "Time to take the cowboys," he said weakly.

"Everybody listen," Buddy said. "One of the cowboys, the one named Drey is a prisoner like the girls and Cook here. As a matter of fact, he is this girl's husband. So let's think a little before going down that way."

Dusty was still holding on to his mother, who could not stop crying. "Thank you God!" she prayed, then said, "My Lord, Missie, who did Andrew shoot today?"

"I almost forgot," Missie said. "He shot Craig, because he said 'Arcadia'. The rules here are no locations are to be told. Mary Ann was not supposed to know she was in Florida. Andrew shot one of Craig's fingers off, and said next time it would be his head."

"That is good to know; at least it will slow him down. Let's several of us head down to the hangar with this young lady and see if we can unite her with her husband." Buddy said, while Tuck called Stella to tell her to come on down.

The sheriff was adamant; he was going down to make sure the cowboys were taken care of.

As Tuck accompanied the crowd out of the house, Buddy and Stephen went into the office, closed the door, and locked it. Buddy called Jerry. "We got her, Boss. The Andrew guy required killing, so we did. But that is not what I called for. I am going to send Josh an e-mail from Andrew's computer. Put me on speaker and get Josh." In a minute, they were all listening, "Josh, I need a short last will and testament of one, let's see here, yes … one Andrew D. Mulhaven. He wants to leave all his earthly goods to his faithful staff—Missie, Mae, Cook and Drey, including his ranch and cattle. Be sure to backdate it for yesterday. Just as soon as we find a signature, I will send it. Ah, my friend, Stephen just found one and I will scan and send it. Better yet, let me send it on this smarter-than-me phone. Can you do that in five minutes?"

"I love it when you ask the simple stuff, Buddy. What do you want me to do the other four minutes? No matter, I'm on it and we are so glad Mary Ann is safe, even sorta glad no one shot you." Josh laughed as he winked at Megan.

"Okay, this is what happened..." Buddy gave them the Reader's Digest version, the main thing being Mary Ann was safe.

****

Jubilation abounded in Lenoir—Buck just sat down and cried, Sherry sat beside him with her arm around his shoulder. The crying offered such relief. Crying and laughing, Sherry said to Jen, "Sit here and help Buck cry. I am calling Robyn and Debbie. They are down in Gastonia praying their hearts out. I told them earlier that it looked like something would happen tonight."

Debbie was with Robyn when she received the call. They shouted with joy. "I will call you as soon as we know more," Sherry explained.

Robyn took the phone. "No need to call. We are headed to Lenoir right now. We want to see Mama as soon as she gets back." Sherry agreed and did not blame them. *I would do the same*, she thought.

In a few minutes, Stephen had the safe open. There were plenty of records of 'sales' and addresses of buyers. There was enough evidence to give the locals and FBI the answer to a lot of unanswered questions concerning missing persons. This was an evidence treasure trove. The will would be embedded in Andrew's computer by the time the Sheriff or FBI impounded it.

There were also stacks of money. Buddy handed Stephen two brief cases and said, "Fill 'em. Take enough to cover expenses and for Mary Ann's pain and suffering. We will let the old MVA board of directors distribute the money as they have in the past.

This cash came from crooks to a crook so there is no legal owner. The government doesn't need it as much as these poor folk who have been held prisoners. If this Andrew had family, he probably has taken care of them royally while denying freedom to hundreds of people." Taking one brief case, he said, "Close the safe but don't lock it. Now let's go recover the parachutes. You check the area out back for Mark David's gear and I will get mine from the second deck. I am sure these brief cases can find their way back on the plane with the chutes and gear." As he finished, he heard Stella coming in overhead.

CHAPTER 20

THE FINALE

Before Stella landed the plane, everyone was in place. The Sheriff looked in the window of the bunkhouse that was attached to the hangar. There was plenty of light and he could see a guy dressed and lying in one bunk. He appeared to be reading a magazine. In another bunk lay the other cowboy. A table had been moved over beside him. A revolver sat on the table with what looked like the remainder of a meal. There was also what appeared to be an open bottle of liquor. That guy's left hand was wrapped in a bloody bandage. *So you are the bad guy*, thought the sheriff as he carefully eased away from the window.

Moving out of hearing distance, he called the men around and explained the scene inside. He assigned two men to take Drey as he came out the door. He figured that would be much simpler than going through the ritual of letting him land the plane. One of the deputies would then hold the light to guide the plane in.

"I want one of you to make it around back to the window. There is only one; it appears to be opened a little. If you have to break it for diversion, do it and be ready to cover us coming in. I will be the first through the door. If he is dumb enough to reach for the revolver, do not hesitate to take him out. He should be a little slow; he may be drunk, but I have misjudged once tonight, and I will not do it again."

The sounds of the engines of the Duke were heard. Talk filtered through from inside the bunk house and then the door opened. The cowboy Drey walked out into the night, carrying the light. It was not switched on. He was startled when the big deputy grabbed him from behind with his hand over his mouth. He started to struggle but the deputy was taking him farther away from the door as he whispered in his ear, "Drey, we are from the sheriff's office. Relax, it is okay. Your wife is here waiting, okay?" Quickly, he nodded and the hand was removed. Sit down over by the door; it will all be over in a few minutes; be cool. The deputy noticed a slight smile come across the cowboy's face. As his eyes adjusted to the night and he could see what he thought was a hundred men in uniform, the smile covered his entire face because Mae, although barely discernible in the distance, was among them, waving. All was well and the nightmare had ended.

The plane dipped and touched down, as if being attracted like a moth to the light, and rolled to a stop. Stella cut the engines. She knew all must be going well when she saw the deputy with the light. But then, from inside the bunk house, she heard a yell. "I hope you cruds brought some liquor! I am about out."

A deputy jerked the door open and the sheriff jumped inside with his pistol pointed toward the man in the bunk. He was followed immediately by a couple men. "Sheriff's Department, you are under arrest. Don't reach for that gun." But it was too late for that. Craig had the pistol, but the glass breaking behind him as the deputy outside hit the window distracted him enough to cost him his life. He lay there in the bunk holding a pistol in his hand that he never got to fire. His eyes rolled back in death.

It was all over, all quiet on the Conestoga Ranch. Yes, very quiet, but there was more happiness in this place than its inhabitants had known for years. Over by the hangar, Mae had made her way to her husband. They were both crying with joy.

Now came the time to wrap up. The sheriff had called the coroner and the rest of his own crime scene team. The team members who'd made it there already took pictures and bagged evidence. Everyone else walked back to the house, allowing the tension to drain out. The chutes and equipment were loaded aboard the Duke. Mark David was going to fly the Duke back to Arcadia, taking Stella to pick up Lear Jet. The powers that be on the ground had authorized it. Drey and Mae had agreed to stay at the hangar to direct them back in. He got the okay from one of the deputies to grab the blankets off his bed, and then went back outside to snuggle with Mae while waiting for the planes to return. They were man and wife but had not as much as touched hands in over a year. There was joy beneath those blankets.

Tuck and the sheriff talked. It was good to have an incident like this end on a satisfying note. None of the good guys were seriously injured. Not many tears would be shed for men who chose in their lives to profit off others' misery. Stephen caught up with Tuck and the sheriff. "We went through and cleared the house; there are no lingering problems as far as we can see. The office looked interesting and, by the way, Sheriff, the safe is open and looks very promising." Stephen got Tuck's attention and with a wink. "I'd bet the computer has a wealth of info inside it as well."

"Yeah, sounds good to me." The sheriff turned to Tuck. "The boys said you were the one that took him out, thanks. He definitely wanted to kill me and, to tell you the truth, I thought he had."

"That musta been your boys but anyway, it wasn't Osama Bin laden, so it doesn't matter."

They walked into the office, which was impressive and neat. At the keyboard, the sheriff hit the space bar to get away from the screen saver. "Well, what have we here? Looks like a last will and testament. The dude must have been expecting an end to his empire. It is a simple will; it says here he is leaving everything to his beloved staff and names them by first names only, but it is his prisoners ... Son of a gun. Uh hum, you guys wouldn't know anything about that, would you? It probably doesn't matter anyway. I have a deputy I can really trust who may find a will with full names on it before the FBI even looks."

"Yeah, imagine that, Sheriff. I can see you are truly a real humanitarian. I could get to like you. Strange, isn't it? The dude had actually accomplishing something good in the last minutes of his life, is that amazing or what?" Tuck grinned. "Can I get a printout of that, Sheriff? It would make a great souvenir? I think our planes will be arriving soon."

"I don't see why not." He hit the print button. "I must say it has been a pleasure working with you."

"Hey, Sheriff, you remember that in the morning when you really will feel like that mule kicked you. It will hurt, I have been there, but you will be breathing. That is what counts for Desoto County and your wife. Rice, I know you don't need the compliments, but you and your men have been stand up guys. I have been meaning to tell you, I was breathing much better after I realized you could handle the curve ball with the speaker at the door and you still managed to get Andrew to open the door, very good job."

"Thanks Tuck, but I am the one impressed. Your team solved a complicated kidnapping in two or three days. Takes a lot of juice."

"I have one last request. I do need to talk to the two couples you rescued from slavery. Do you have a problem with that?" Tuck asked.

"Not at all, the living room should work. I will get everyone together. And send a car down to get the two lovers. One of the deputies will relieve them operating the landing lights," he said, smiling. It wasn't but five minutes and everyone was there.

As quickly as he could, Tuck explained why he and his friends were never here. He reiterated that the sheriff came out to make the arrest and rescue. We just helped. With the sheriff's blessings, he also explained that the ranch would be theirs. But it would have to go through the courts and that sometimes takes a year. "Talk to the sheriff and I am sure you will be able to live here until things are settled. I am sorry about it, but you guys will be questioned until you are tired of it. There are so many questions that will have to be answered. Records here show that there are hundreds of people just like you living somewhere as slaves to some sleaze balls. It has been lovely meeting you and seeing the smiles of freedom. Pay attention to Sheriff Wise; he is a very good man to have on your side. He could have died attempting to rescue you tonight, Andrew did shoot him. If he wasn't wearing his protective vest, Andrew would have killed one more before he died. I would venture to say the only real good thing that your Mr. Andrew ever did was writing that will."

****

Goodbyes were said. Mary Ann promised to come and visit and bring her Buck for them to meet. "I just want to say, you two girls are precious; if you need anything that I can do, or you just want to talk, call me. You have my number."

"Speaking of Buck, I have got to call him. I need your phone, Dusty."

"Anything for you Mama, anything. You have never looked better!" He gave her the phone and hugged her again.

"BUCK, it's me! I love you! And you had better ask me to marry you when I get home. I have missed you, you big hunk."

The phone conversation continued as they walked out to the planes. The planes headed for Sarasota. They dropped off the Duke, Informing the authorities they were returning the plane to Mr. Thompson. Inside there was an envelope containing twenty thousand dollars of Andrew's money. The paint job was not very good and it would need to be redone. The serial numbers would need correcting. There would be something left to cover the worries over a missing plane.

The packed jubilant plane continued its flight on to Lenoir and the Lower Creek Airport in the Lear Jet 60. The whole crew heard Mary Ann's story it was so wild if they did not know Mary Ann it would sound like fiction. Every few minutes Mary Ann would sound off, "I can't believe you found me. When I saw Dusty I knew it must be a dream. How did you find me?" They were all about to dance, the air was electric.

****

At the little airport cars had to be moved over to the side. There hadn't been this much action at Lower Creek Airport since it was commissioned.

The Sheriff was there to see the end after Billy had called him. Billy and the Lenoir crew had already gotten the story during the flight. Mary Ann's voice had been sent via satellite to the command center. At the command center she was put on the speaker for all to hear.

There was jubilation and anticipation, knowing this event was ending perfectly. Their plans, dedication, cooperation and expertise had proven once again that the MVA could still function when needed. As all the boys and girls would say 'Life is Good'.

As Stella did her magic and landed the plane with more weight than she had ever had aboard, there were yells, screams, tears and just jubilation as she did a one eighty and taxied back to the crowd. Matt and Luke ran out to set the chocks and give Stella the thumbs up and she cut the engines.

Family and friends were waiting. After hugging her daughters and talking, waving and speaking to friends, she walked over to Buck. They hugged and Mary Ann whispered, "You are last to be hugged, big boy, but this is forever if you want it to be."

The more they talked, the tighter they hugged. "I

have missed you like crazy," Buck said, teary-eyed. "I thought I had done something wrong. I want you forever, Mary Ann. ... Will you marry me?"

Mary Ann turned to the crowd that stood transfixed, watching the love show. "He asked me to marry him, and I am saying YES! This man is my hunk! And we will never be separated again!"

Yells and cheers echoed through the mountains of North Carolina. Mary Ann looked around and thought—*how wonderful it is to be free.*

The After Glow

Only a few weeks after the happy reunion at the small airport in Lenoir.   There was at a small wedding in the foot hills of the Blue ridge Mountains.. Mary Ann wanted Sherry for her Matron of honor. There was joy at the 'Chapel of the Field' where Buck and his best man Russell were standing with the minister waiting for the bride's appearance. Russell leaned over to buck and whispered, "Remember Buck, no children." And they both had a good chuckle.

The excitement was building, Russell whispered again as Mary Ann started down the aisle, "Son if you die now the mortician will have to break your face to remove that smile."

Buck thought, *How right you are Russ my friend, how right you are. She is beautiful.*

Mary Ann was the beautiful bride. It was a simple ceremony, until the minister asked Buck if he took Mary Ann as his wife, Buck answered loudly with a grin, "You Bet!"

Then came Mary Ann's time and her answer, "What he said, YOU BET."

The small chapel was packed, and laughter rang out. An indication that this was going to be one happy senior couple.

Mary Ann and Buck live and love on top of the mountain and every day give thanks for family and friends who can always be counted on to be there when they are needed.

ABOUT THE AUTHOR

The author has served honorably in the USMC, USAF and the USN. He retired from the USN as a Chief Petty Officer, where his last assignment was teaching Naval Intelligence Processing. He is a Licensed General Contractor, a professional   chalk artist and story teller. He And his wife   have appeared from   Cuba to Canada.   They have entertained audiences of thousands and groups of three or four. Together they have appeared and taught at Youth Camps, seniors groups, churches and BSA functions. After hundreds of original stories he has put some of his ideas on paper.

He and his wife, Sherry, at in their mid 60's, took a break from traveling in the motor home and hiked 1850 miles on the Appalachian Trail. This hike lead from Georgia and ending for them at Franconia Gap in New Hampshire. Leg injuries prevented completing the final 300 miles. Since then they have returned to the Trail. They still plan to finish, a little at a time.

He and his wife still travel full time in their motor home where he now writes the stories he has told over the years and some of the ones he has dreamed. Life to them has always been an adventure. That odyssey began September 1956.

About the authors books

"Sticky"

I loved this book. I got it yesterday and other than sleeping, I spent the last 24 hours reading it. It was a great mystery, plus a romance and gave a lot of information about new technology and even some history of the last frontier! (Alaska) I will reread again. It is definitely worth reading! L. Mitchell, Kansas City, Missouri

****

"Rags"

I have read every one of Tom Clancy's and John Grisham's books. Your book was just as spellbinding if not more so. I do want to purchase the new book. Of course, I will want a signed copy...... Nathan, PLS Rutherfordton, North Carolina

****

"Gracefully Grasping for Dignity"

I read the book...."Gracefully Grasping for Dignity"...and found it very informative....I would recommend it to any family who find themselves in the place of having to make a decision one way or the other about their parents welfare....or spouses....or children!!! Ora, The Chaplains wife, Kentucky

****

"Why Not Forever"

..............I loved your book "Why Not Forever" which I

finished last night!! It's most unusual for me to finish a book that quickly - but it was such interesting reading. Love the way you laid out the advice on sex, dropping little hints early, and using it to tantalize the reader to keep reading....The chapter or section which was most meaningful to me had to do with your advice to seniors about the old question of re-marriage after the death of the spouse.

Bishop Fred Brannen, Missions Administrator, former missionary

Other books by the Author

Toby's Tales

A children's book about a turtle born in the desert and travels to Texas. His tales are tall, but good over his one hundred year life.

S'Gar (Just say Esgar)

Mystery novel of a modern vigilante group who serve out justice to the bad guys who use the law to get away with dirty deeds.

Excerpt......

Take a look at the book 'Finally Love', The book where the love story of Jerry and Sherry began. It is NEVER too late for happiness.

FINALLY LOVE
CHAPTER 1

"Have I waited too late? I have spent my life looking for satisfaction in medicine, excitement and challenges. Now? Yes, now, Jerry, you think of love." Jerry ran his hand through a shock of salt and pepper hair and sighed. He looked out his massive office windows to survey the panorama of Pittsburgh and the mountains and tried to put his life in perspective. No one would argue that his life had not been a full one. His life had been mostly highs--from the Head of Medicine at Duke to CIA operative "Doc" — till he hit bottom after the one "black op" that went crazy. Then he went AWOL and lived as a hermit in the woods near the little town of Mt. Bell, NC. He befriended a stray dog he called Satan while he fought his mental demons. It was during that low point in his life that four boys changed his life. They had tagged him "Rags." To them, he had seemed a bum of the most intriguing and elusive caliber.

Jerry turned to pace across the room. He remembered the accident and how, in saving the life of one of the boys, his own life had been saved. The demons of his depression were conquered and he got a new lease on life. He left the life of a hermit and returned to the family business in Pittsburgh. In his absence, good friend and company attorney, Dallas Fletcher had turned the family business into an international business worth billions.

Finally Love

Jerry's blue eyes smiled back at him from the mahogany-framed mirror. This was the part of his life's story he always enjoyed recounting. After returning to Pittsburgh, he achieved the crown jewel of his successes-the MVA. It was his dream, it was his baby. It was the Modern Vigilante Association. Organized and managed by Jerry himself, the MVA existed to mete out justice in those cases where regular law enforcement simply could not. The MVA circumvented certain laws that seemed to protect the criminal. Jerry took pride in safeguarding the integrity of the MVA. Projects were taken on a case-by-case basis. No one man decided which projects were accepted; it was always a group decision, and the group had been handpicked by Jerry, all men of integrity and outstanding character. One of the most important safeguards was that Jerry reserved the exclusive right to disband the MVA at his discretion, and it would automatically be disbanded in the event of his untimely death.. Jerry did not want the MVA to be a self-perpetuating entity that could potentially grow to be an arm for misjudging or for personal gain. Initially Jerry funded the venture with his personal finances, but over time some money came in from projects the MVA took on. In cases such as drug operations in which complications prevented proper return of money, the money was simply used by the association to fund the next "event." The MVA had been an exciting and rewarding mistress. But like the rest of Jerry's action-packed life, she left no room for a real love.

Jerry looked at himself in the mirror. Seventy years old, still tall and erect, still handsome, but high time to remedy the situation of no love. He paced back to the window and stared at the mountains in the distance. The now disbanded MVA had accomplished what it set out to do. The successes and accolades were more than he could count from memory. Even more rewarding than the projects themselves was watching the four special boys become men and work hand in hand with him in his life's centerpiece. Jerry smiled as he remembered seeing young "J" fall in love with the cowgirl. Then knowing that Sticky had found love and still had time for work in the MVA, caused an even larger smile. Okay, come to think of it all the boys had found time for romance and love while still putting their best efforts into the MVA. Tuck got Rose; Buddy had found his Di in the United Kingdom while on a job there. "Where did I go wrong? Could I have actually had a life and accomplished what I have?" He knew that he was asking a rhetorical question. He heard himself laughing out loud. "How would I know?" He paced back to the mirror and started rearranging the three pots of orange bromeliads that sat on the credenza below the mirror. "Improvise, adapt, overcome. Improvise, adapt, overcome," he repeated as he shifted the flowers. No, it was late, but not too late.

Despite his apprehension, Jerry knew his next step was the right one. He had not talked to Sherry since the "event," but tonight he had a date with her. The "event," which he mentally referred to as "THE Event," was an MVA event that regrettably took down Sherry's husband.

"Well, not regrettably, either. The fool deserved it," thought Jerry. After the MVA event, Jerry had felt the impulse to go to Sherry, but found the whole situation too awkward. Fortunately he had Dallas, dependable Dallas, who had flown down to speak with her. He remembered the conversation when Dallas returned.

"How's she taking everything?" Jerry had wanted to know.

"Surprisingly well. Brady's death was a blow to her, but in some ways I think she suspected trouble was coming. Her life with Brady was a living hell, and she's actually relieved to be free of him."

Finally Love

Jerry tried to examine his feelings. Yes, he was glad she was doing well, and no, he couldn't separate that from the irrepressible feeling that he had just struck it rich in life's gold mine of opportunities. Jerry had never lost his feelings for Sherry since their days at Duke University. He had always pushed the feelings to the back burner of his busy life. He couldn't help feeling that life was handing him a second chance.

"Don't blow it, you old codger," he told himself. He decided to give Dallas one more call before he left.

"Dallas, did you arrange to have my car waiting at Douglas?"

"Jerry, is that you? I have never failed to make your arrangements."

"I know. Sorry."

"Are you okay?" Dallas asked. "I don't think you were this uptight when Smith Electrical threatened to sue our pants off!"

"I know, but that was easy: I just let you handle it, Dallas."

Jerry heard Dallas' reassuring laugh. "Hey Buddy; I'm behind you all the way on this, too. Besides, Sherry will make you feel at home. Call me anytime you need me."

"Thanks, Dallas." Truly, he had been more confident of what to do when he was on a high stakes mission with the CIA.

His driver was waiting in the parking deck, and Jerry headed down. In short order, they were at the airport. As the plane gained altitude, Jerry watched Pittsburgh grow smaller and smaller. Back to Mt. Bell! His minded wandered back to the last time he had been there.

He had learned much in his time spent in the woods of Mt. Bell as a hermit. He had learned humility. He had been called names, and there were times on the street he knew he had been intentionally avoided. Ah, but then, there were times of solid friendship, especially that of Father O'Shields. Jerry looked out the window. They were well above the clouds now. The Father was a learned man with a couple of doctorates and years of experience with fallen men. "Father O" could look past the surface and see deep within a man's tortured soul.

In complete contrast to Father O was his wonderful down-to-earth friend Mrs. Harris. She had befriended him at his lowest point. He had met her early on a cool fall evening as he walked the railroad tracks into the little town of Mt. Bell. There she was, buying apples from the "Apple Man." The "Apple Man" had set up his little business just off the tracks down town where the railroad split the town in two. He kept a fire going in a tin tub to warm by as he hawked the North Carolina mountain apples. Mrs. Harris looked at Jerry as if she knew he carried a heavy secret. She smiled gently.

"Have an apple, North Carolina's best! If you ever need anything or even just to talk, drop by my house. Two blocks up, one house over. The house with the long steps on the back porch."

She avoided telling him that her son was the chief of police. She knew people well, and she knew that fact would give him cause not to visit. Jerry smiled a sideways smile every time he remembered that older lady with the cute pug nose. Truth was he had stopped by her back porch with long stairs many evenings. Sometimes it was to share stories of her family and a piece of her "stacked apple pies." Most nights it was to hear her warm motherly voice; it had been a comfort, a real soul comfort. His own mother had died while he was young, and he grew up without a mother in his home. Mrs. Harris never sought to pry into his life,

Finally Love

but seemed happy just to be a friend. That was when Jerry was known as Rags, but Mrs. Harris never referred to him by that name.

Now Jerry was not Rags, he was also no longer S'gar, he was Jerry Wiley again, and he was headed to Mt. Bell and a date. This was actually the first personally social date of his life; he felt like a kid, and here he was seventy plus years old. He sat listening to the sounds of the jet pushing itself toward Douglas Municipal Airport in Charlotte. His mind was crowded with conflicted emotions. "This is silly." "No, it's right." "I'll look foolish." "What do I have to lose." "Should I call Dallas?" "She's an old friend..."

His thoughts were brought up sharply, "...whose husband you've killed."

There was *that*. He hated to think of it, but he did all the time. Brady deserved what he got. Looking back he knew logically that there had been no other way. Brady had been cooking the books of his medical practice. He had a small clinic. The maximum logical amount of income was two mil a year, but he was passing fifty million through it. Sherry also worked at the clinic and knew there was something wrong but was too emotionally abused to attempt to do anything about it.

When the problem of drug trafficking in the Southeast first came up, the Omega Clinic was a big red light. At that time Jerry was notified that the owners were old classmates of his (Drs. Brady and Sherry Oxnard). He looked into it. The more the troops dug into Brady's past, the more it became apparent that the business in the small town of Huntersville could not produce that income. The obvious sources were checked: insurance, Medicare and Medicaid fraud. The clinic came through like a champ. The clinic had even given some free services to needy individuals. (It didn't surprise Jerry to learn that all the pro bono work was done at the direction of Dr. Sherry Oxnard and not her husband.) On the basis of what the MVA gave to the state, an investigation was started by the State Department of Drug Enforcement. But for some reason, within a few weeks, the clinic was given a clean bill of health, nothing wrong there.

Thinking of that result, he had to smile again. Dr. Simpson, heading the investigation, did not know the tenacity and abilities of the MVA staff. Within a few hours they knew Simpson had deposited fifty thousand dollars in his offshore account. It did not take long to connect the dots with what they already had. What came from the MVA investigation was the fact that the Omega Clinic was financing a local supplier. The clinic was cleaning the money when the product was sold and writing checks for perfectly reasonable services that were never performed, for equipment that was never delivered.

The MVA board met and made the decision to take the rogue doctor down. They were going to give him a back door to exit, allowing him to keep some of his ill gotten gains in exchange for turning on the supplier, in effect shutting down a huge amount of drugs on the East Coast. The plan was developed by the inner circle, S'gar, Tuck, Buddy, Sticky, and J. Buddy was elected to go inside, something he loved. He was the most likely pick since he had been so long away from that area.

Jerry could see the MVA event as though it were yesterday. It had gone as planned. Buddy infiltrated as a misplaced runner coming in from Texas. The cover fit his history. They had picked a guy who would conveniently disappear, giving him a perfect backdrop. He was accepted fairly quickly as a mule from Miami to the Charlotte area. With his expertise he had developed a rapport with the supplier. He soon became the go between with the doctor.

Finally Love

The MVA had removed the other intermediary from the equation along with $100,000, thus giving the appearance of a greedy runner doing a disappearing act. He was held in a very secure place unharmed but making several tapes, later to be turned over to the North Carolina Narcotics Task Force and the Federal Drug Enforcement.

The final day, the take down day, had started out normally. Buddy was supposed to meet with Doctor Brady Oxnard. The majority had agreed that Brady would cave in when confronted with the facts. Buddy had entered the office. That is the very moment the first sign of trouble appeared. S'gar along with Josh, Tuck, and J were in a van with all the monitors going when Josh said, "Oh no, we have lost audio. It is recording, but not amplified."

Normally in a case where it was expected, they would have had a lip reader, but no one had anticipated the need on this event. Josh was methodically trying to solve the problem. Everyone else was watching the video feed.

S'gar, "At least it looks like it is going well." The meeting had just started. They pieced together the dialogue later from Buddy's report.

"Ah, Dr. Brady my man, how was your day?" Buddy asked

"Just give me the money, Hatch. I have had a busy day and don't have time for small talk." stated the doctor in his condescending tone.

"Well Doc, as you already know you are under investigation …" Buddy was cut off.

"Can it, Hatch. That is over. We paid that fool Simpson; he settled, fifty thou. That was chicken feed, and that is fixed, but what has that got to do with you?" the doctor said with a confused look on his face.

"To borrow a line from several books and movies, I am your worst nightmare. I am the undercover guy who is going to hang your rear; you are on candid camera now. You just admitted to bribery of a state medical investigator. Now let me list your options," said Buddy calmly, but he was interrupted.

"There is something you don't know. Everything leaving this office is jammed. No one is getting anything!" And he reached into his center desk drawer. At the same time Buddy saw a figure coming at him from his left through a side door. His instincts told him "bad guy, GUN." That put guns to his left and in front.

Instantly, he kicked the desk forward, ruining the aim of the doctor. At the same time, he fired two quick taps from his silenced weapon at the center of mass of the figure at his left, all without taking his eyes off the doctor. He knew the man at his left was down and out.

"Don't be stupid, Doctor. Put it down; you still have a chance," but before he could finish, to preserve his own life, Buddy had to fire his silenced Glock. There was no chance for the doctor. He died almost instantly.

"Did you get that?" He spoke into his mic. As he was speaking, he turned and saw his team enter.

Explanations were made about the sound. As they were talking. Josh came into the room. "Here is the tape. The sound is good; it was a glitch with the input feed. It is clean as you requested — no prints."

Finally Love

"Okay, sanitize the office, then everybody out of here," said S'gar as he laid the tape on the desk. Rubber gloves covered his hands. Everyone was busy under Buddy's directions, wiping every place any of them could have touched. The bodies were left as they fell. S'gar picked up the phone, dialed 911, placed a small box over the mouth piece and spoke to the operator, "This is Dr. Brady Oxnard. Shots have been fired at my clinic. You will need drug enforcement personnel." He hung up as the operator was asking his name.

The office used had outside entrances. S'gar wanted to talk to Sherry, but that was not possible then. He remembered how his heart sank as they drove off. A block down the road they passed the police vehicles, lights and sirens ablaze, headed to the Omega Clinic. "*Omega* is the end, right?"he thought as they continued down the road not exceeding speed limit.

The murders were never solved. All of the data gathered by MVA was anonymously delivered to law enforcement. That, along with the runners' confessions and testimony, helped seal the fate of the supplier. Sherry was not held or charged. The workers at the clinic testified in her favor, and even the supplier himself said, "That dumb broad don't know nothing. She woulda sunk us a long time   ago   had   she   knowed   anything."

She willingly made her statements about her instincts, which were telling her something was wrong, but her husband never discussed money matters with a woman. It was beneath him and above her head, he had said.

****

Jerry had sent Dallas down to talk to Sherry. Dallas conveyed

Jerry's condolences and offer for any personal or legal help he could provide. Jerry also asked Dallas to put out a feeler to find out if Sherry was open to a call from Jerry. Her response had been immediate.

"Certainly, I would love to hear from Jerry."

****

After all the court cases were disposed of, and the possibility of Sherry having to testify was all in the past, Jerry bolstered his nerves and gave Sherry a call. Now he was a man on a mission. He wondered if Sherry could see him as more than a concerned friend. He hated that he could not put a realistic measure of the chance of succeeding with her. Every other mission he had engaged in was carefully calculated, and chances of success carefully weighed against potential failure. Here there was none of that. He simply had no way to know.

"Wheels on the ground in ten minutes, Mr. Wiley." The pilot's voice brought him back to the present. He could not get some folk to call him Jerry in a professional setting.

"Thanks, Elsie, it was a smooth ride as usual."

He made a quick trip to the head and freshened up. Then back and buckled in. Elsie made a smooth landing and taxied to the private rental hangar. His car was already there. Dallas had arranged everything. Jerry noticed a beautiful bouquet and a box of Miesse chocolate on the seat.

"Thanks, Dallas, you think of everything," Jerry thought. He started the engine and the correct address appeared on the GPS. "Wow, I am a lucky guy." Taking a deep breath, he engaged the transmission.

Chapter 2

Finally Love

Jerry turned the black Impala onto Wilkinson Boulevard and headed west toward Mt. Bell. He passed the places he used to walk in the evenings when he was called Rags. What used to be the Imperial Mill Village where he had spent many an evening talking with Mrs. Harris was now the new development of Hawthorne. He noted the upscale houses and carefully landscaped yards. It seemed out of place in a way. The entire village of wooden lap-sided "mill houses" had been torn down or moved to be replaced by the new brick homes. Sherry had picked a beautiful setting to which to return. He parked in front of the address he had been given. He tried to place the house in relation to where the houses used to be. For some reason this house seemed to be in or very near the exact spot of Mrs. Harris's house.

"I hope this is a good omen," he thought.

The afternoon was beautiful. The Knock Out roses were still blooming furiously, and the maple leaves were just starting to show the first hint of autumn color. He rang the door bell and adjusted his collar once more with the hand that held the bouquet. The door opened almost immediately. Sherry looked lovely in a short-sleeved royal blue sweater that showed off the best highlights of her wavy gray hair. Awkwardly he tried to hand her the bouquet through the storm door. They both laughed, and she opened the door and invited him in.

As the door opened, Jerry was assailed by the aroma of sticky buns. He was transported to meetings of the MVA when they all enjoyed the unparalleled perfection of sticky buns made for them by Sticky's mama.

"Come in. Make yourself comfortable. I'll get some water for the flowers. Such pretty autumn colors! And Miesse chocolate. How delightful! Thank you."

Jerry looked around at the open, but homey décor. Dallas was right. He felt right at home.

In just a few minutes Sherry reappeared with a tray of coffee and the sticky buns. "Coffee?" she asked.

"Yes, thanks."

"Sticky buns?"

"Thanks, they smell great!" said Jerry. "You know sticky buns originated in Pennsylvania, but they're just called cinnamon buns there."

"Really, even the ones with nuts?" Sherry asked.

"No kidding."

"So what other strange things do you Pennsylvanians do? What else have you been up to? It's been so long since I've seen you."

"I've been in Pennsylvania for a while with Wiley Industries."

Sherry said, "I've often wondered what happened to you. It seemed you disappeared off the planet after you resigned as head of Duke."

"Those were the days," Jerry replied. "I see you're still sporting team colors."

Sherry looked down at her sweater. "I did not even think of that!" She laughed, and Jerry thought, "Her laugh is the same; I've missed so much."

Finally Love

"Do you have family?" she inquired.

"No, I've been married to my work. It's time for a divorce, though."

Sherry laughed obligingly at his wit. "I don't have family either. But I'm actually rather enjoying doing things my own way for a change. And actually Mr. Fletcher told me you didn't have family."

"And what else?" wondered Jerry to himself.

As if reading his mind, she volunteered, "Mr. Fletcher had a lot to say about you, said you were an honest guy, but that you had been involved in a lot of secretive things. He said more than once that you were on the side of justice and that you were honest." Sherry chuckled, "If you ever need to promote yourself, Dallas is the guy to do it. He mentioned that you had even lived in Mt. Bell for a while. But no one around here remembers you living here," she added significantly.

"It was very nice of you to offer legal help and condolences when Brady died, but it seemed very unusual to hear from a lawyer all the way from Pittsburgh just out of the clear blue," Sherry said. She paused to adjust the orange and bronze bouquet Jerry had given her. He sensed that she was waiting for an explanation. He had the sensation of being on a merry-go-round that was going ever faster with no safe way to dismount. He watched her small fingers touching the flowers in the vase and he saw himself earlier in his office arranging the pots of flowers and saying, "Improvise, adapt, overcome." He would have to improvise and adapt right now because this was moving faster than he ever anticipated.

"I'm so very sorry Sherry, this is not going the way I hoped.

There is so much involved, years and years of water under the bridge. I wanted to get into it slowly, but I know that is impossible. Please hear me out, and then if you want, I will leave."

"Oh, Jerry, I have every intention of hearing you out. I promised Dallas I would give you a chance, and I assured myself this is too much high drama not to know. There is so much to catch up on, and we have plenty of time. I didn't make reservations. Here in Mt. Bell, if the restaurant is too busy, we just go to another. It's not Pittsburgh or New York City and the Club 52. So let me warm your coffee, and you go ahead with this tale."

Yes, Sherry, I did live here in Mt. Bell, or more accurately, just outside. But first I need to talk about the CIA." Sherry said nothing, but he saw her jaw drop as her lips silently formed the letters C-I-A. "The CIA approached me about working for them. What person doesn't want a little excitement after fourteen years of study and all medical stuff?" Jerry went on to explain that after his involvement in a couple black ops he was hooked, so he resigned as head of Duke Medical, and went full time as 'Doc' with the CIA. He told her of the death of a child in one of the ops that went bad and how it sent him into depression.

"I knew I was in depression; after all I am a doctor. I just walked away. But in the mean time my dad had passed away, and I went back to the business for a few months. I turned it over to Dallas, gave him full rein, and let him drive it. I never checked on the business, just assumed it would stay about the same without me."

Jerry paused to take another sip of coffee. "Wow, this is great coffee!"

"Holy Cow," said Sherry.

"What?"

"That's the brand of coffee. Holy Cow Coffee Company from out in California. I really like it, myself. But, please," she

Finally Love

motioned for him to continue.

"Anyway I walked away; I went AWOL from the CIA. The only place I could think of was Mt. Bell. When I was small Dad had known Mr. Stone and bought a large piece of land here. So I made my way here and lived in the woods." Smiling at the thought he continued, "I became known as Rags, the bum. I developed a nice little cave to live in. Father O'Shields at the Abbey loaned me a goat, and I found an injured dog, nursed him back to health and named him Satan. I liked being with Goat and Satan. They were comfort. I needed them to talk to, and they were so good at listening." They both laughed.

"I became involved with four boys, from a distance, who were determined to bug me. The encounters were enough to irritate me. When they were in my vicinity, I kept a distant vigil on their activities. Soon I realized they were just being boys. Then I started to see how they played dangerously at times, much different from my structured childhood. Looking back I realize that I associated them with the kid who had died in the black ops. I became paranoid, very protective of the boys from a distance.

"Then the thing I feared happened. One of the boys almost drowned. Well he actually did drown, but I pulled him in, and after much ado, I performed open heart massage and saved his life. But my life of RAGS was over, over in more ways than one. There in the bed of an old pick-up truck, holding that twelve-year-old heart in my hand changed my life instantly. I was no longer a depressed bum, but an alive doctor, saving a life. All of a sudden I realized, 'Jerry, it is impossible to save them all, but saving one is worth everything.' I did not save the kid in South America, but by God, I was going to save this one. Thousands of ideas raced through my mind as I kept perfect rhythm with the heart. I had a new goal in life; I wanted to help folks who could not help themselves, not always with medicine, but in many more ways. The operation was a complete success. A scared man took us to a clinic in that old beat up truck. There we were transferred to an ambulance and headed for Gaston Memorial Hospital. A dream was developing.

Order any of Jack's books on line as an e-book or paper back...

www.ingramcontent.com/pod-product-compliance
Lightning Source LLC
Chambersburg PA
CBHW022146170626

46807CB00005B/2100